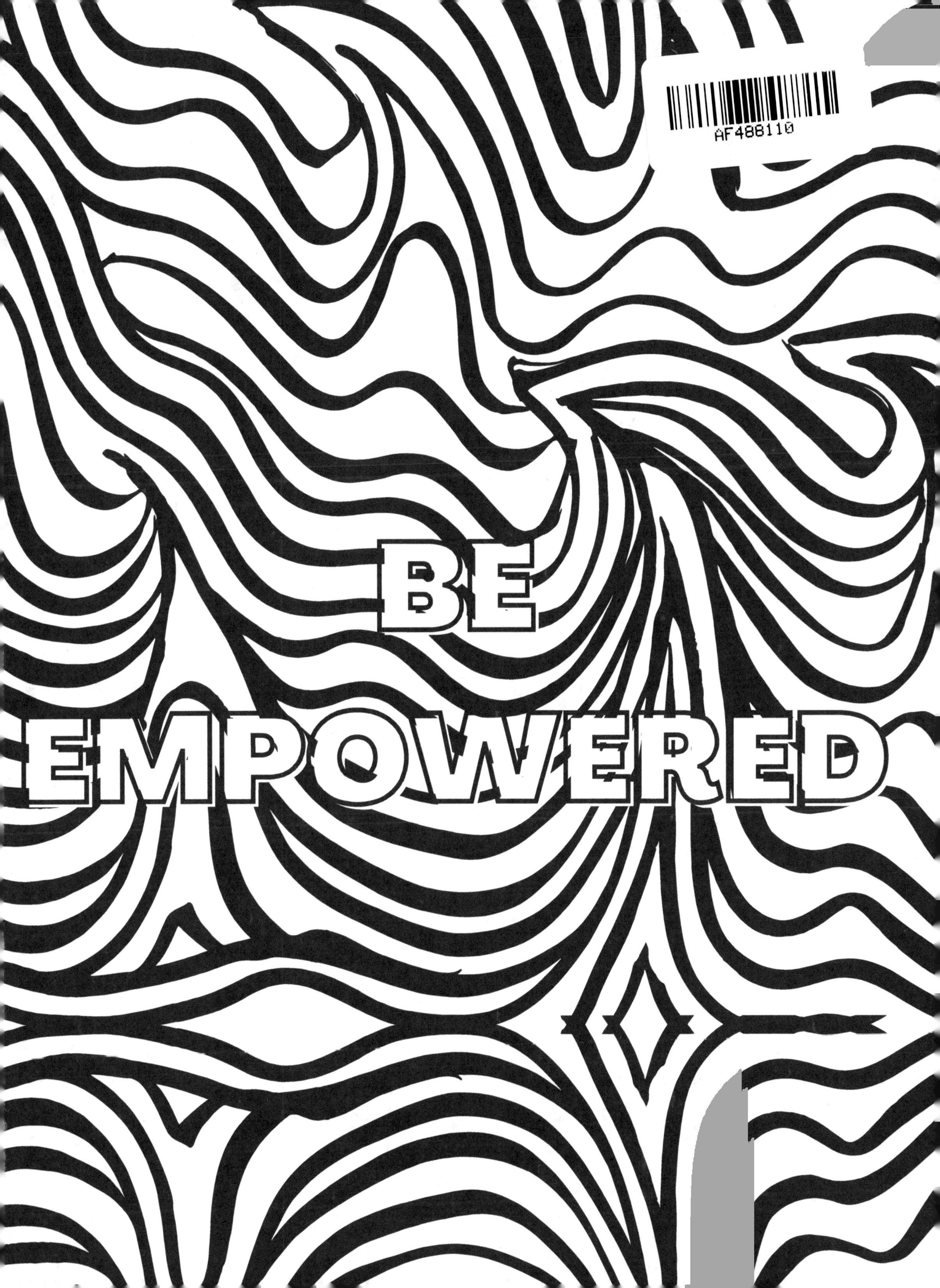

AF488110
BE
EMPOWERED

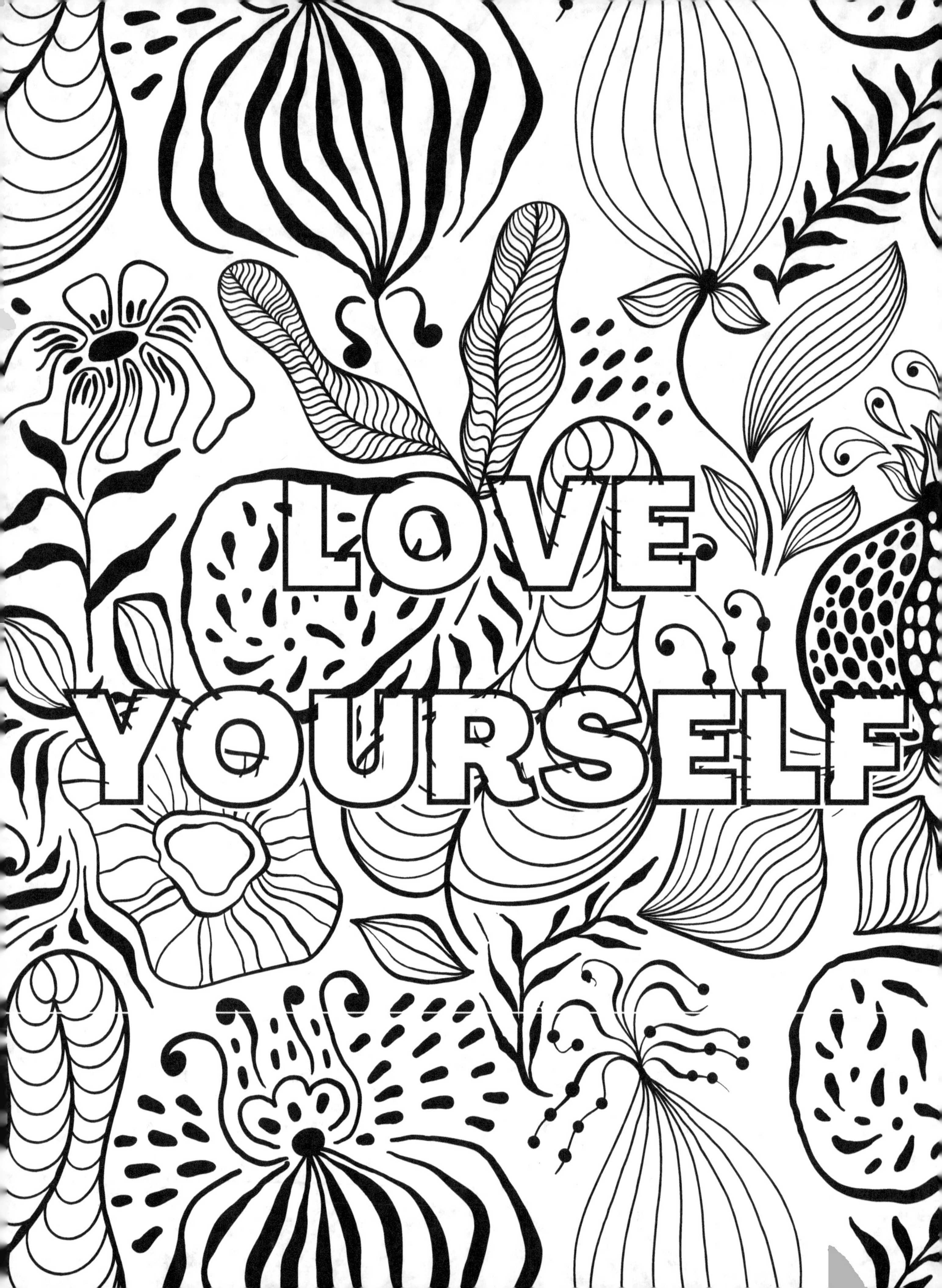

LOVE
YOURSELF

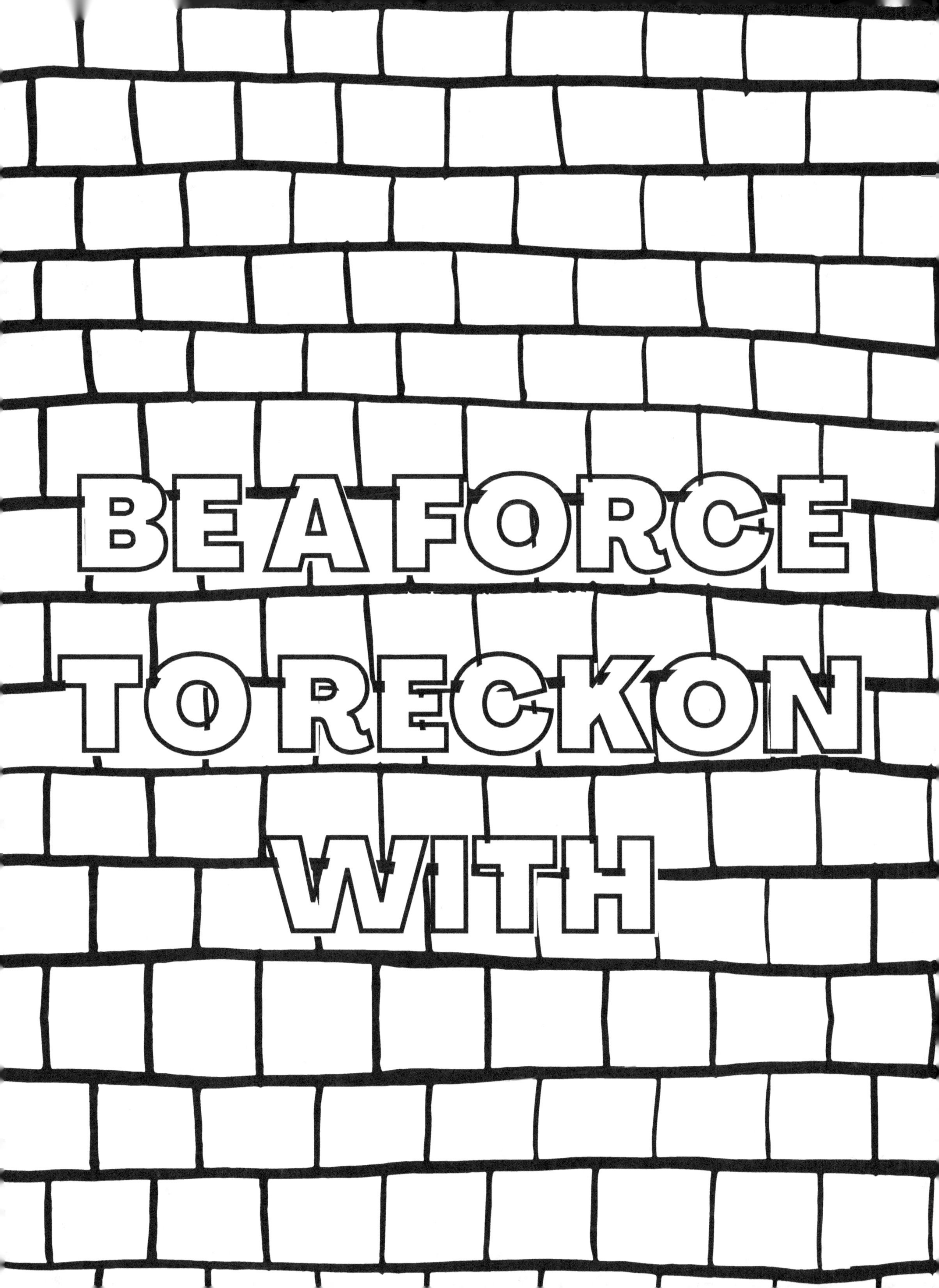

BE A FORCE
TO RECKON
WITH

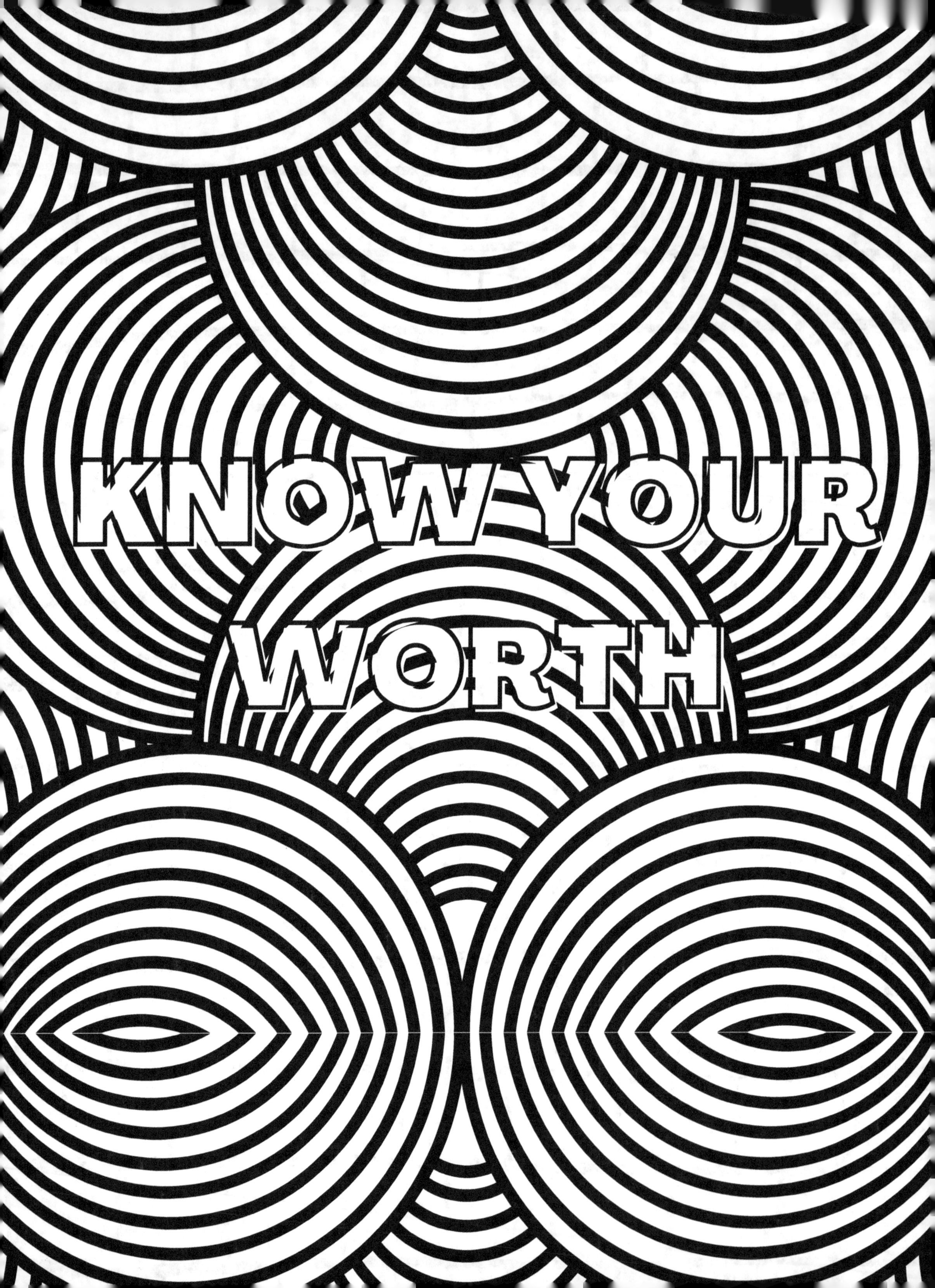

KNOW YOUR
WORTH

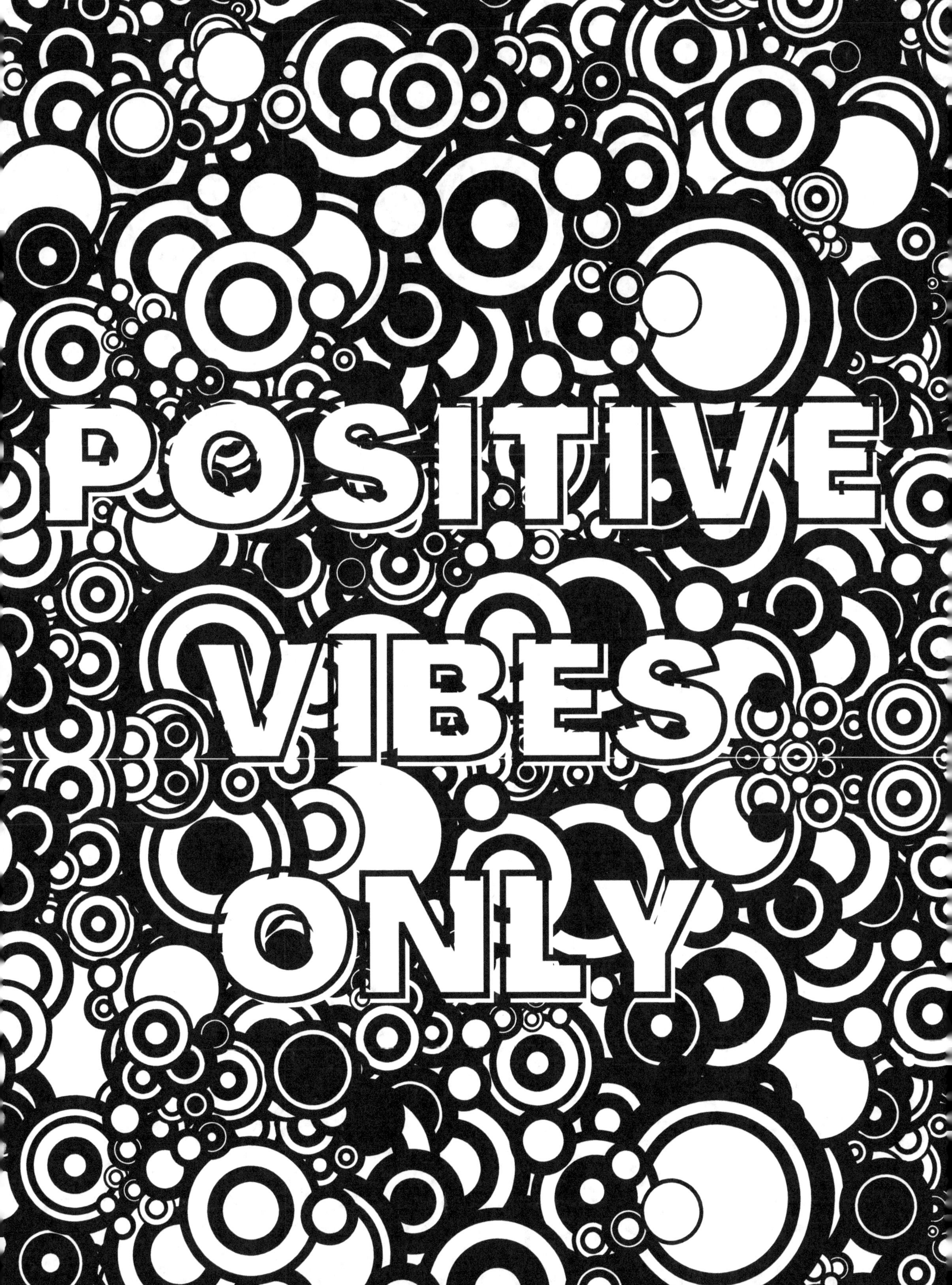

POSITIVE
VIBES
ONLY

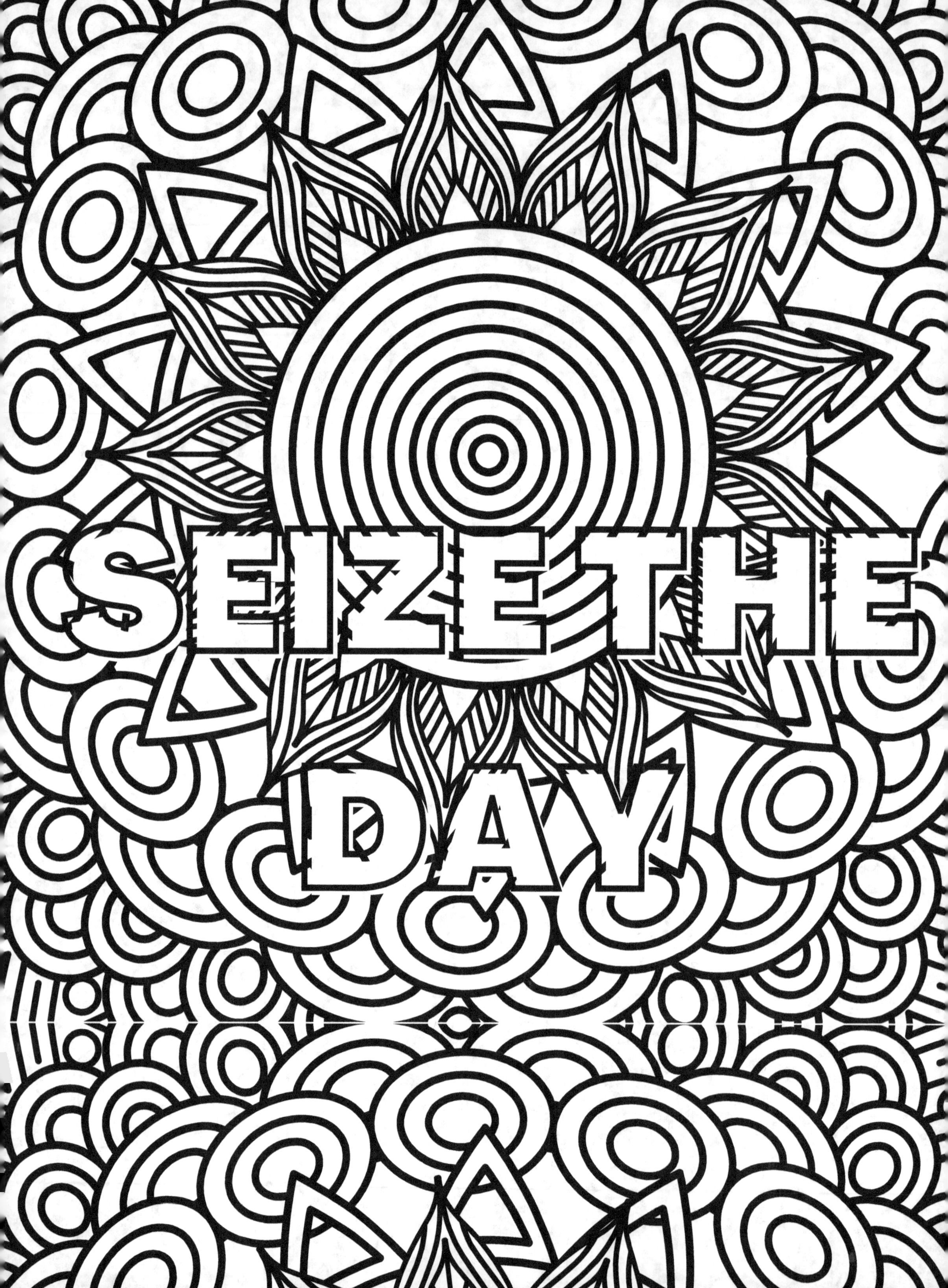

SEIZE THE
DAY

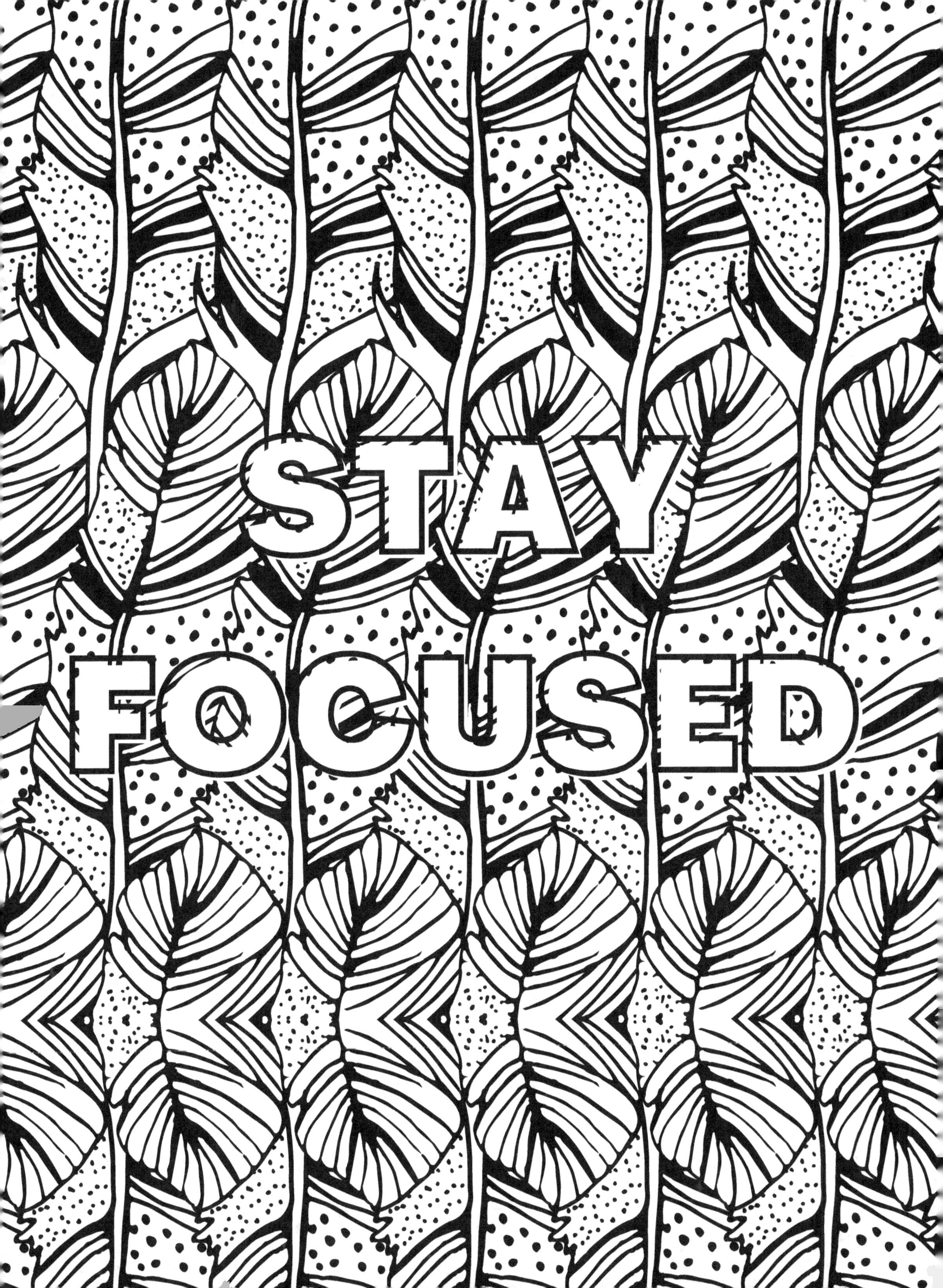

STAY
FOCUSED

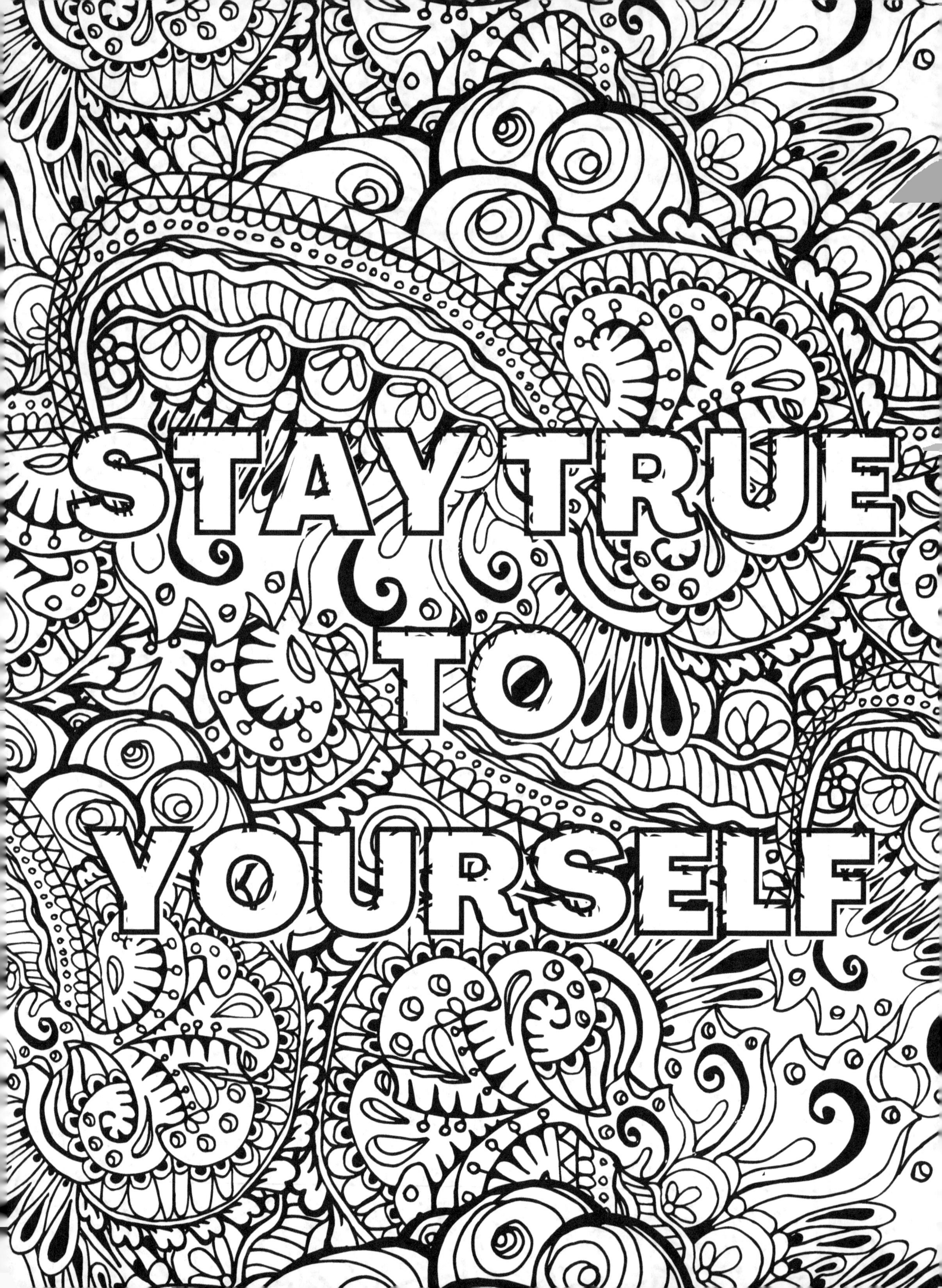

STAY TRUE
TO
YOURSELF

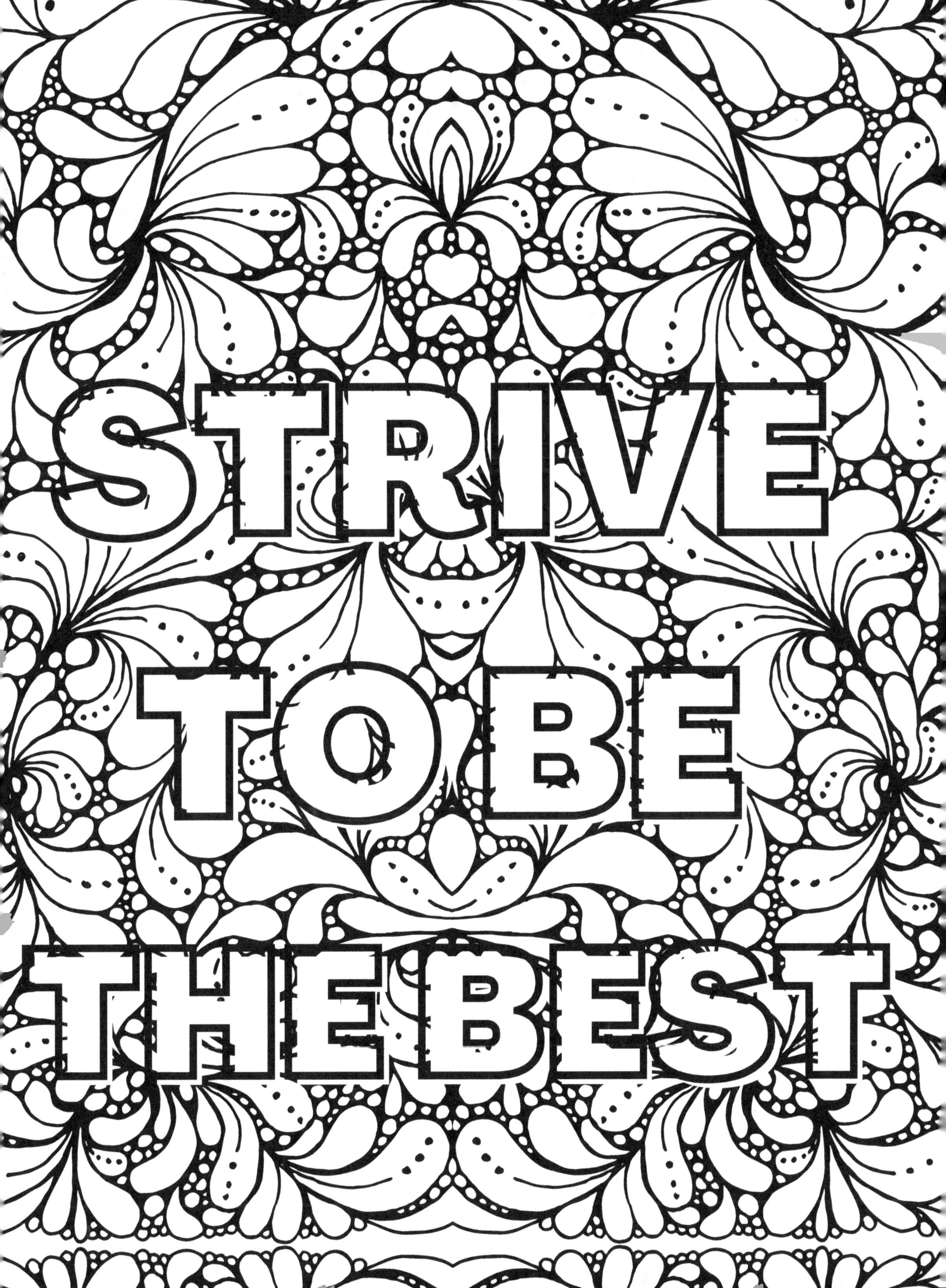

STRIVE
TO BE
THE BEST

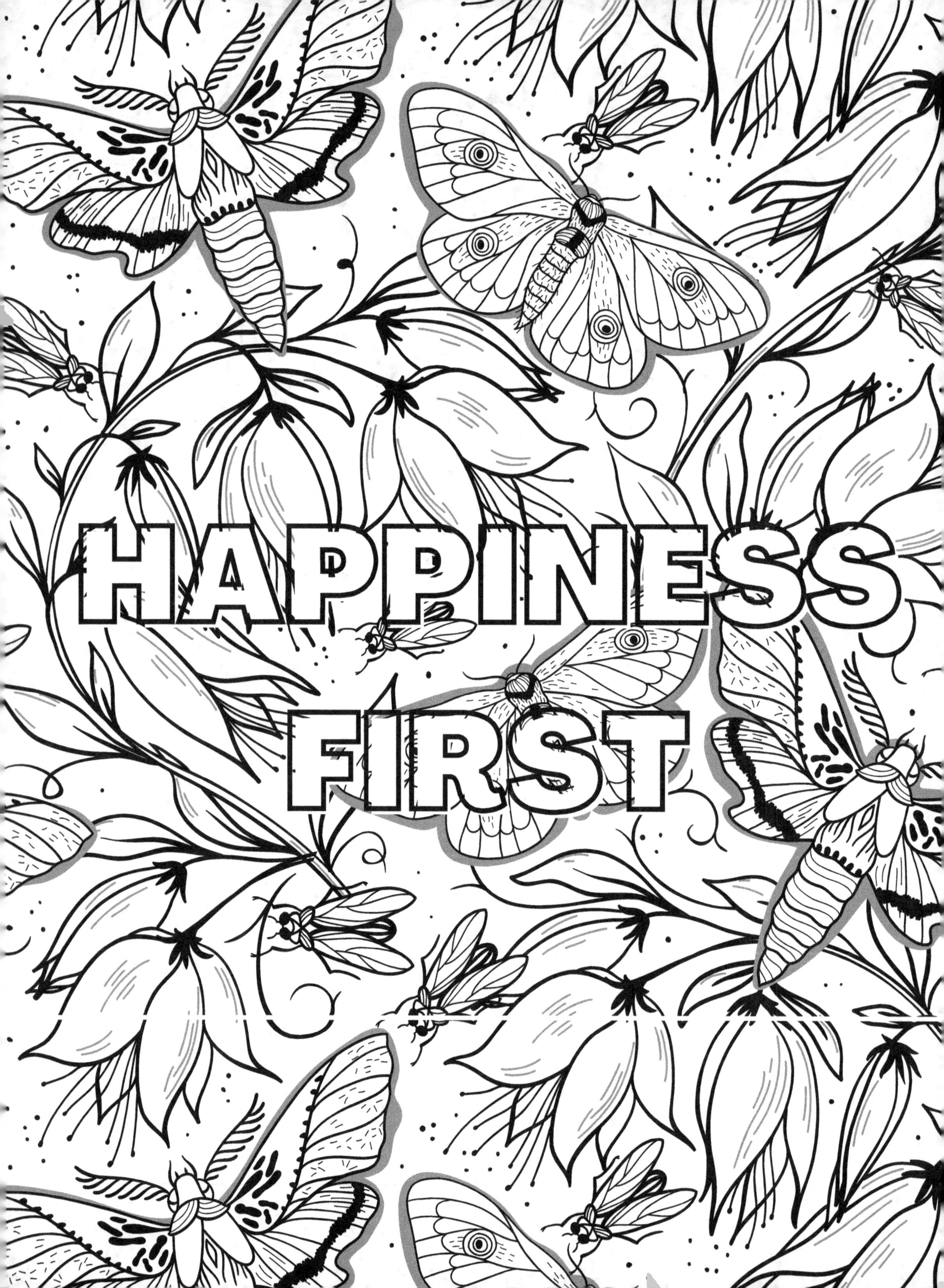

HAPPINESS
FIRST

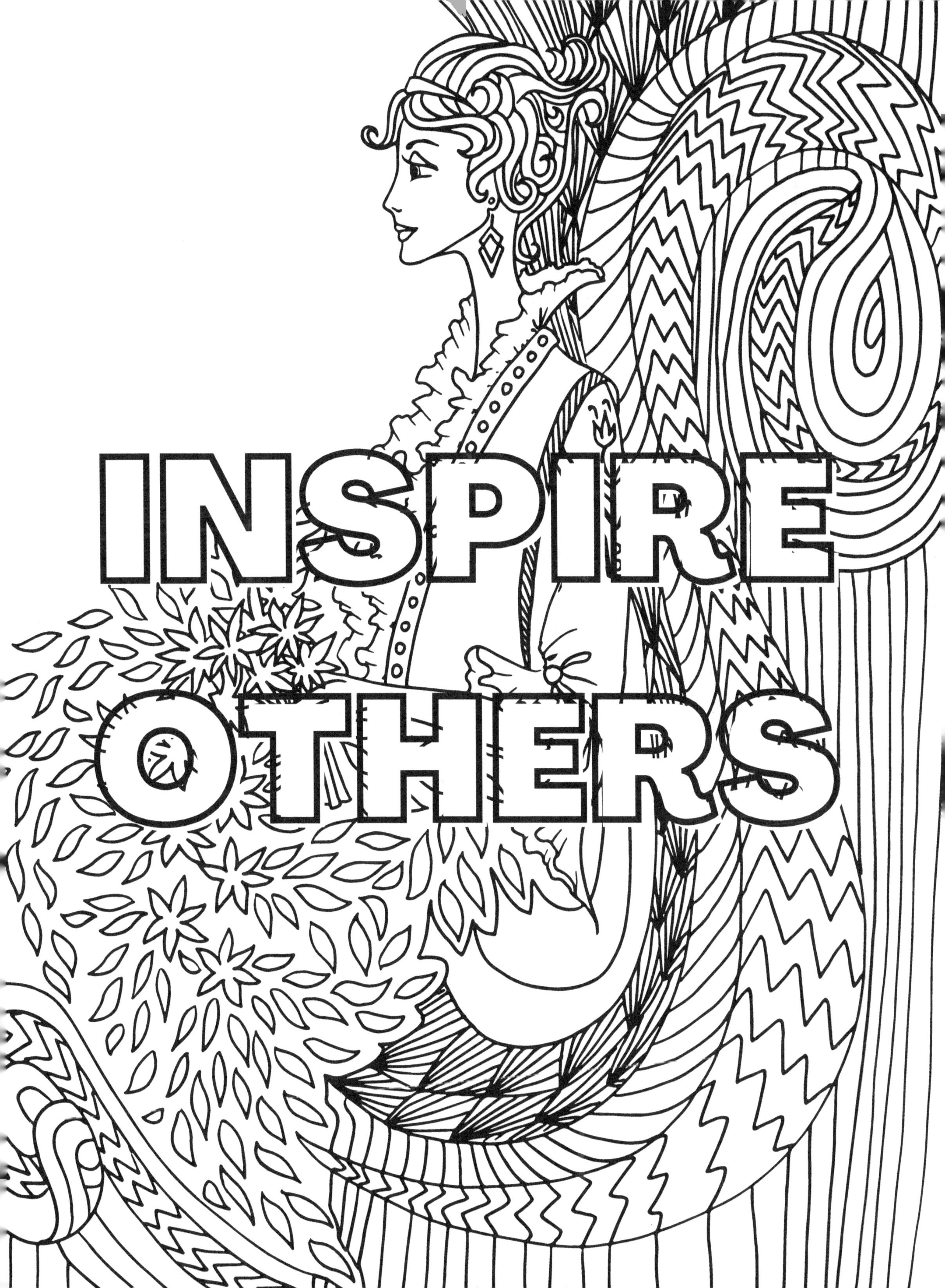

INSPIRE
OTHERS

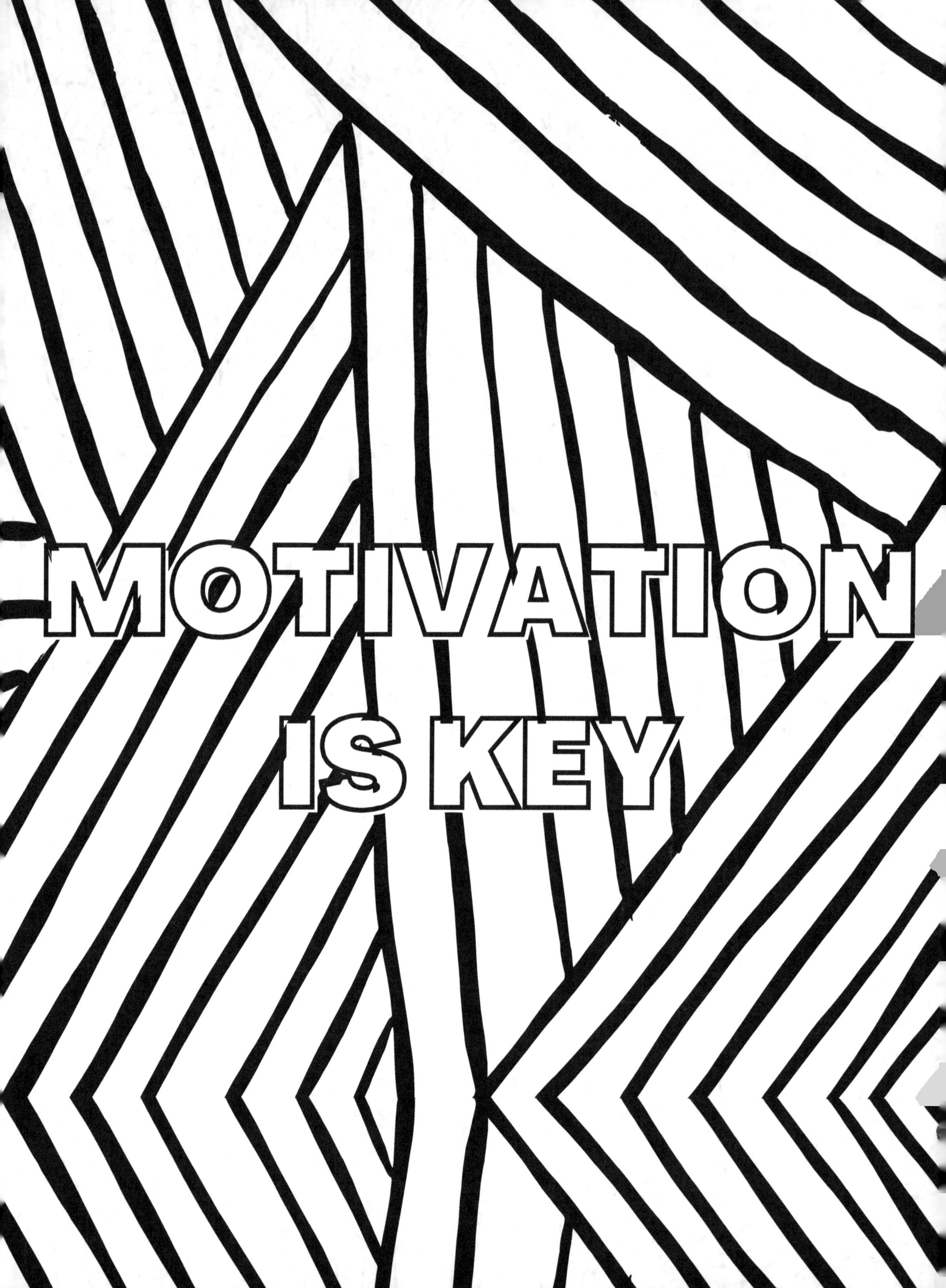

MOTIVATION
IS KEY

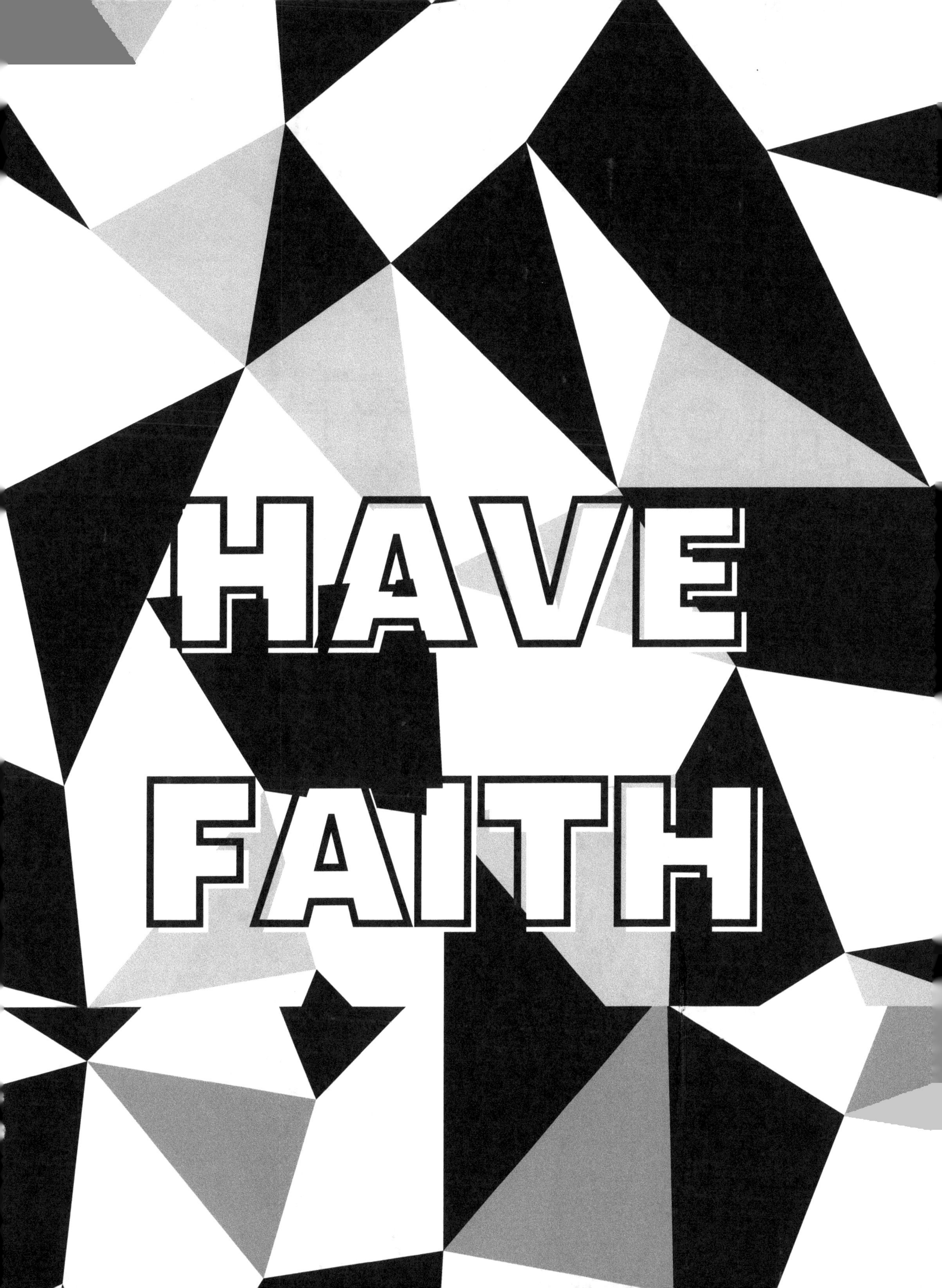

HAVE
FAITH

HONESTY IS
THE BEST
POLICY

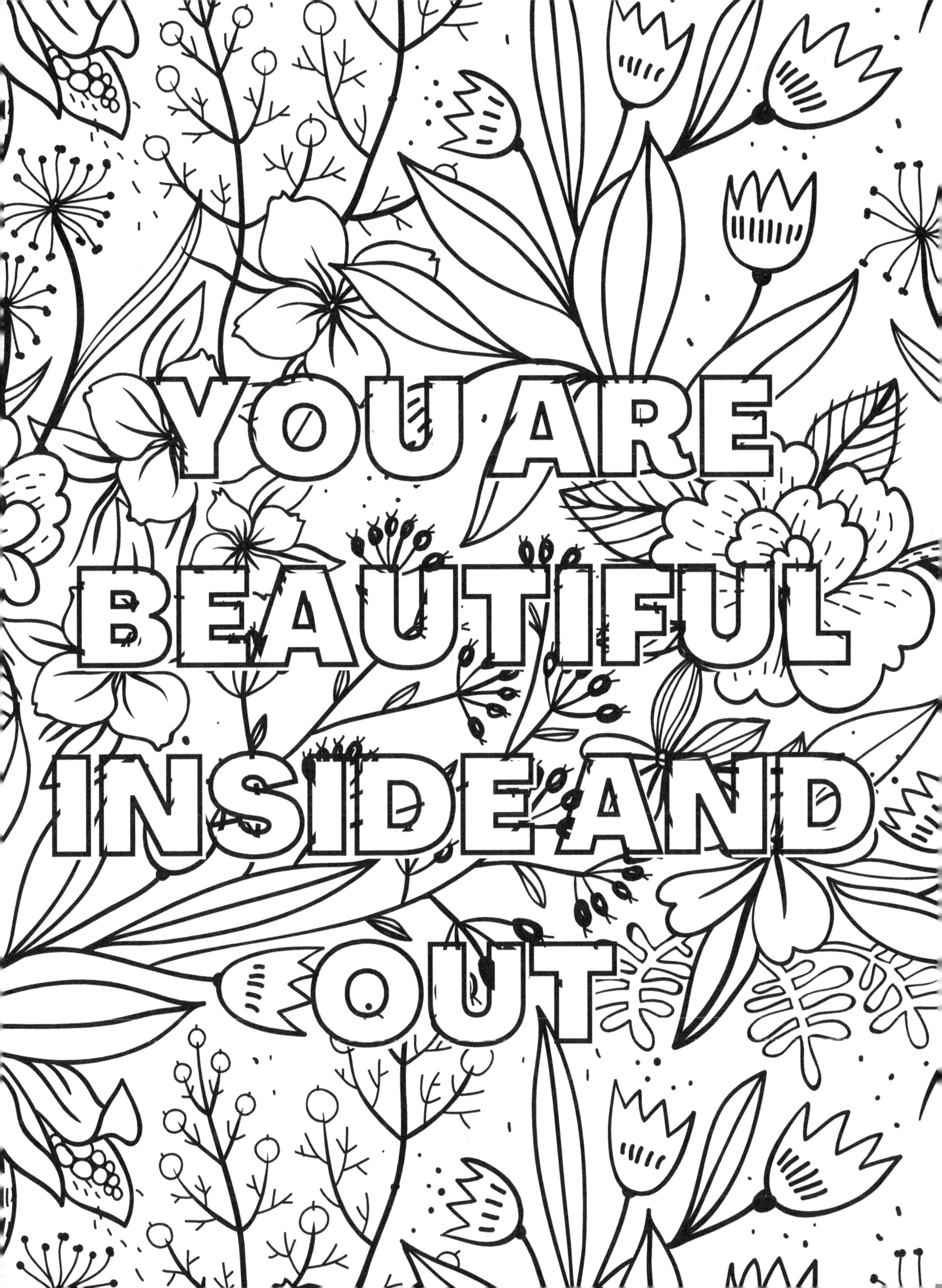

YOU ARE
BEAUTIFUL
INSIDE AND
OUT

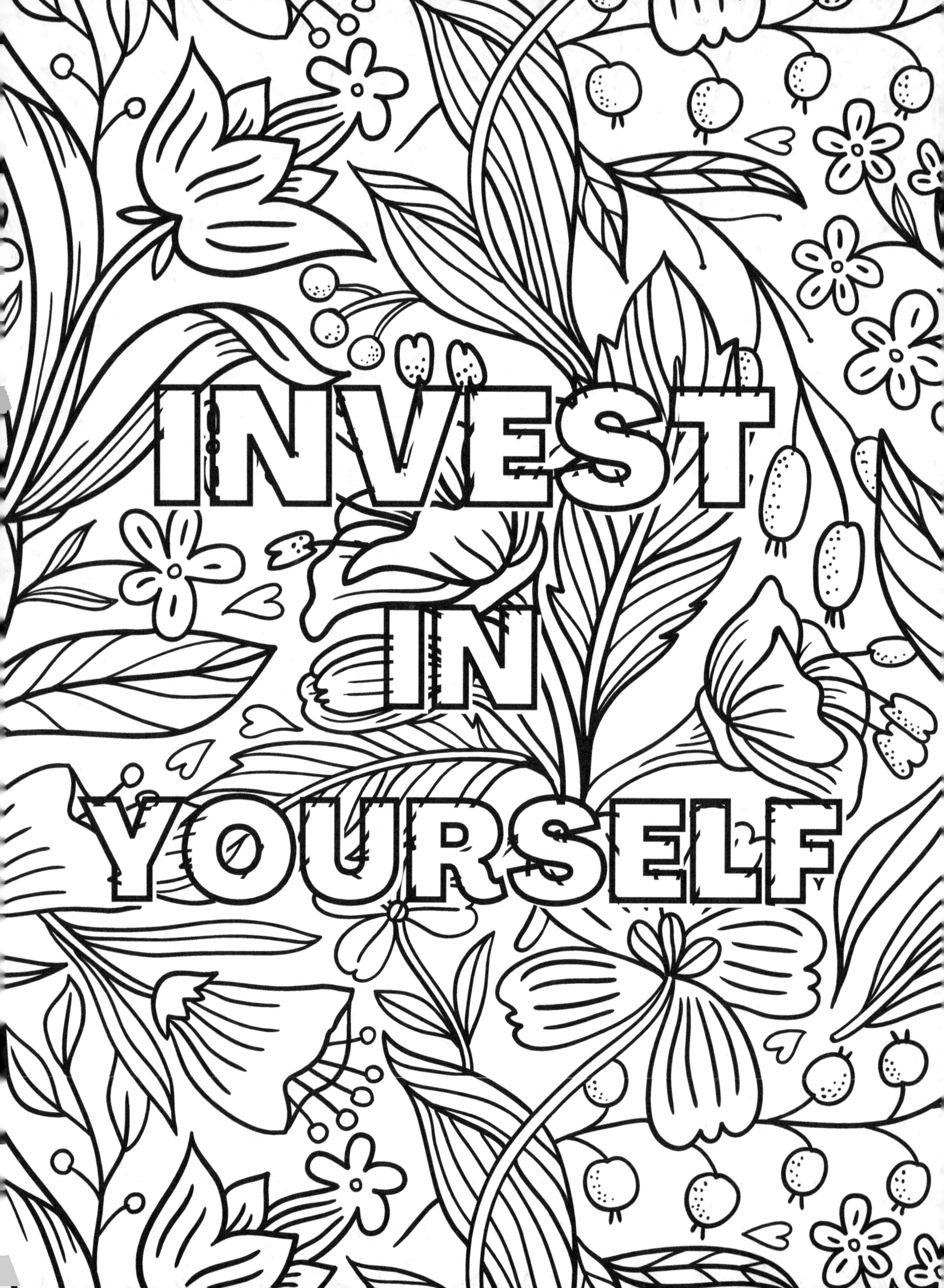

INVEST
IN
YOURSELF

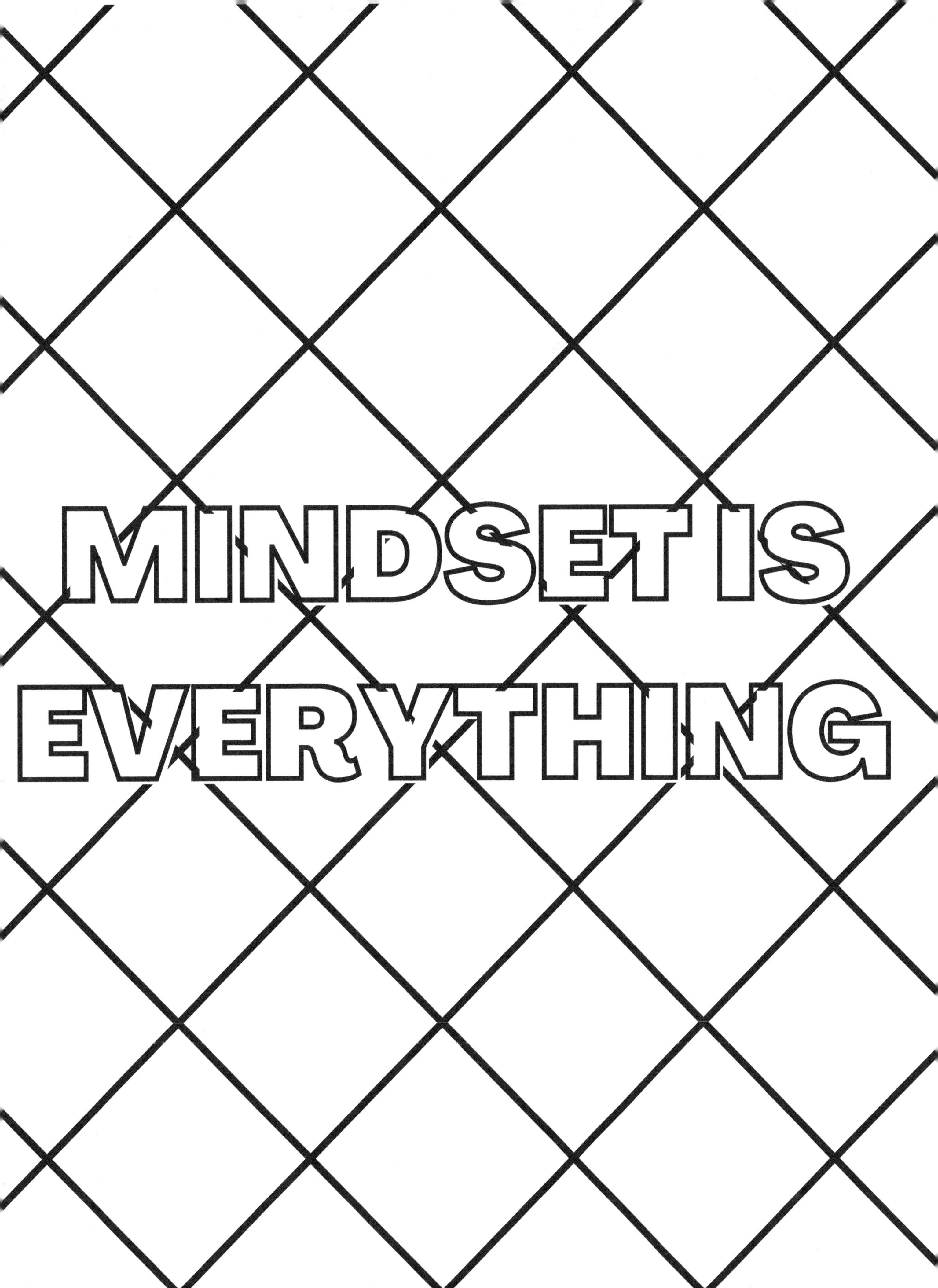

MINDSET IS
EVERYTHING

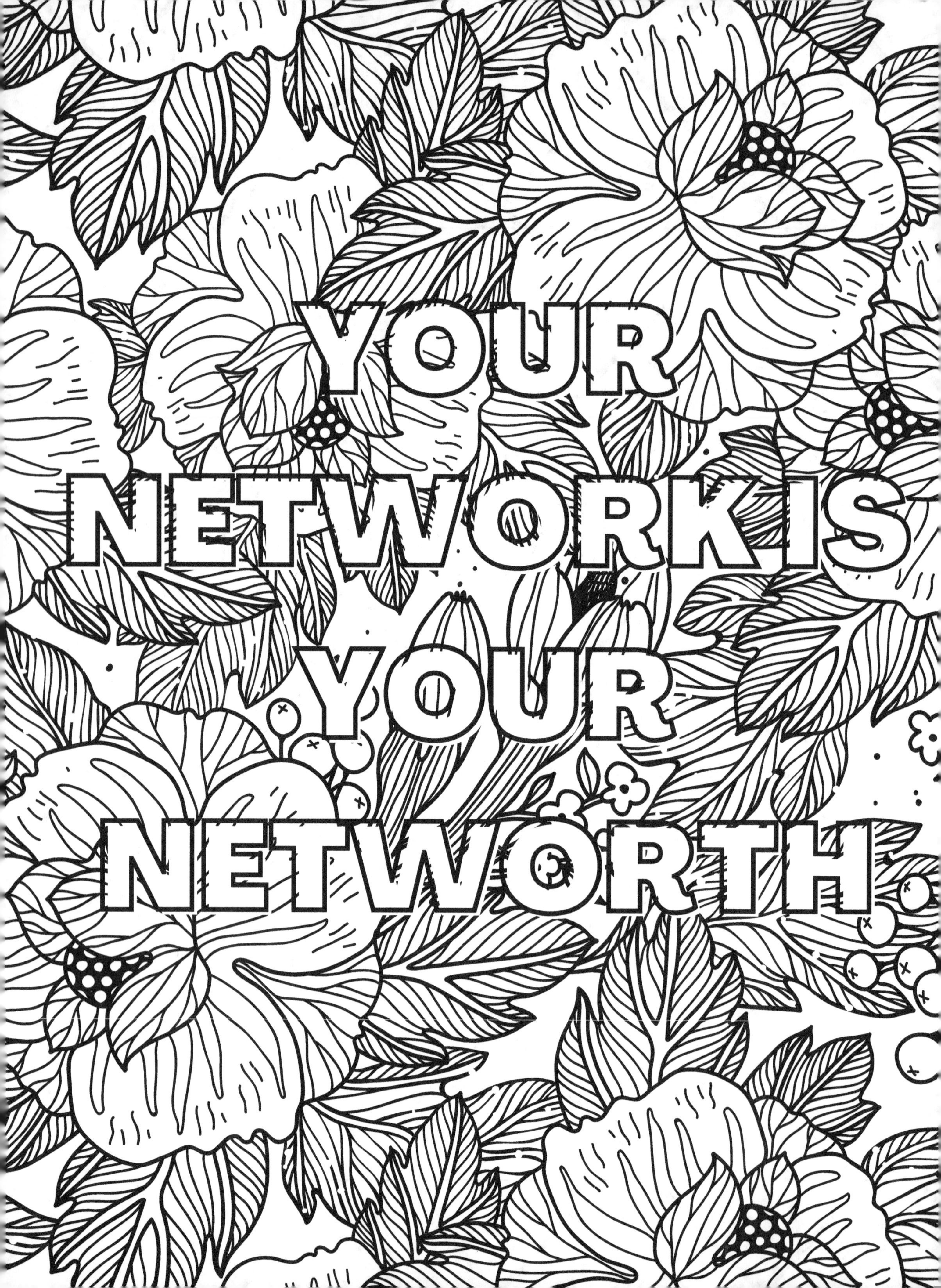

YOUR
NETWORK IS
YOUR
NETWORTH

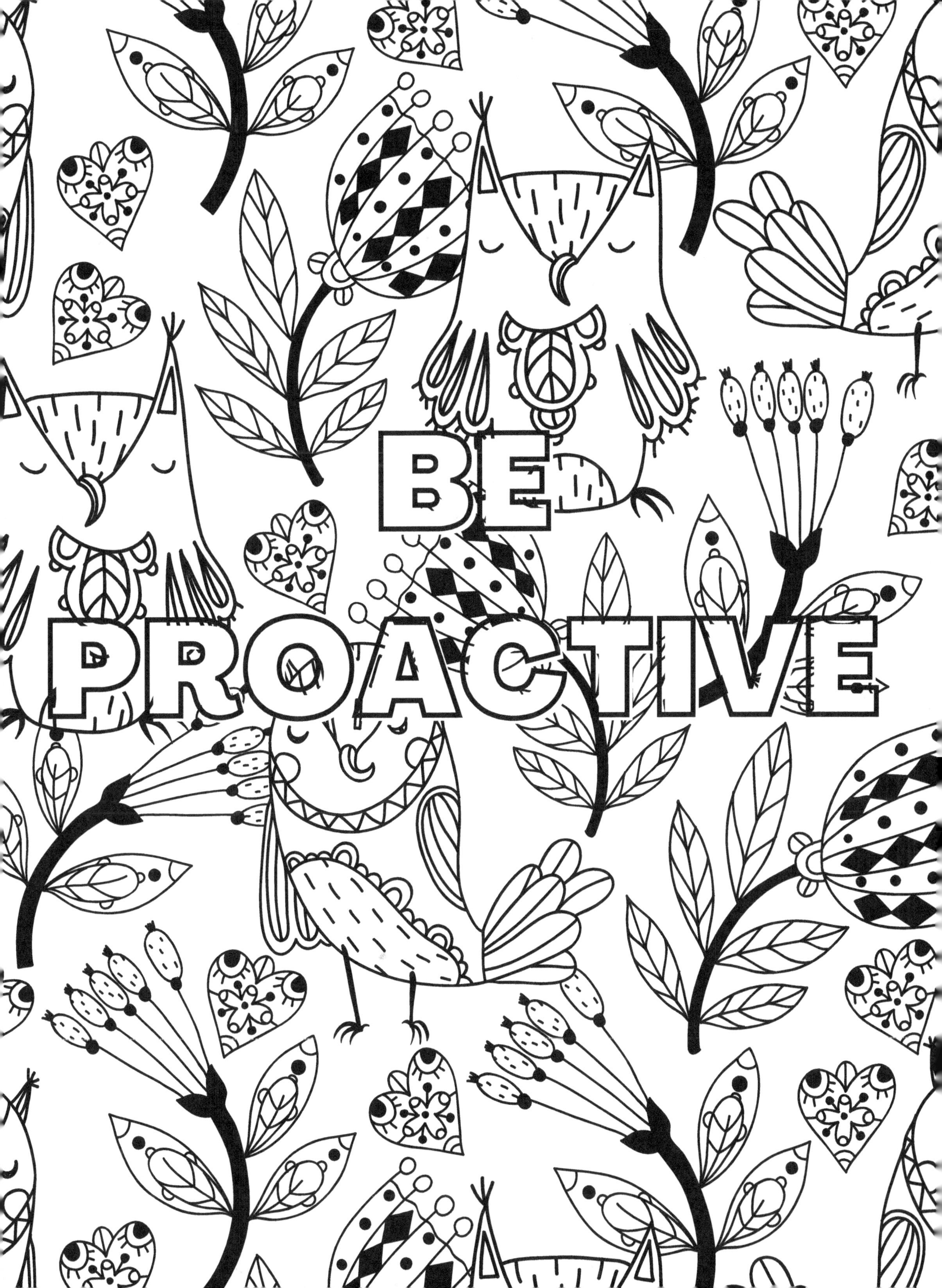

BE
PROACTIVE

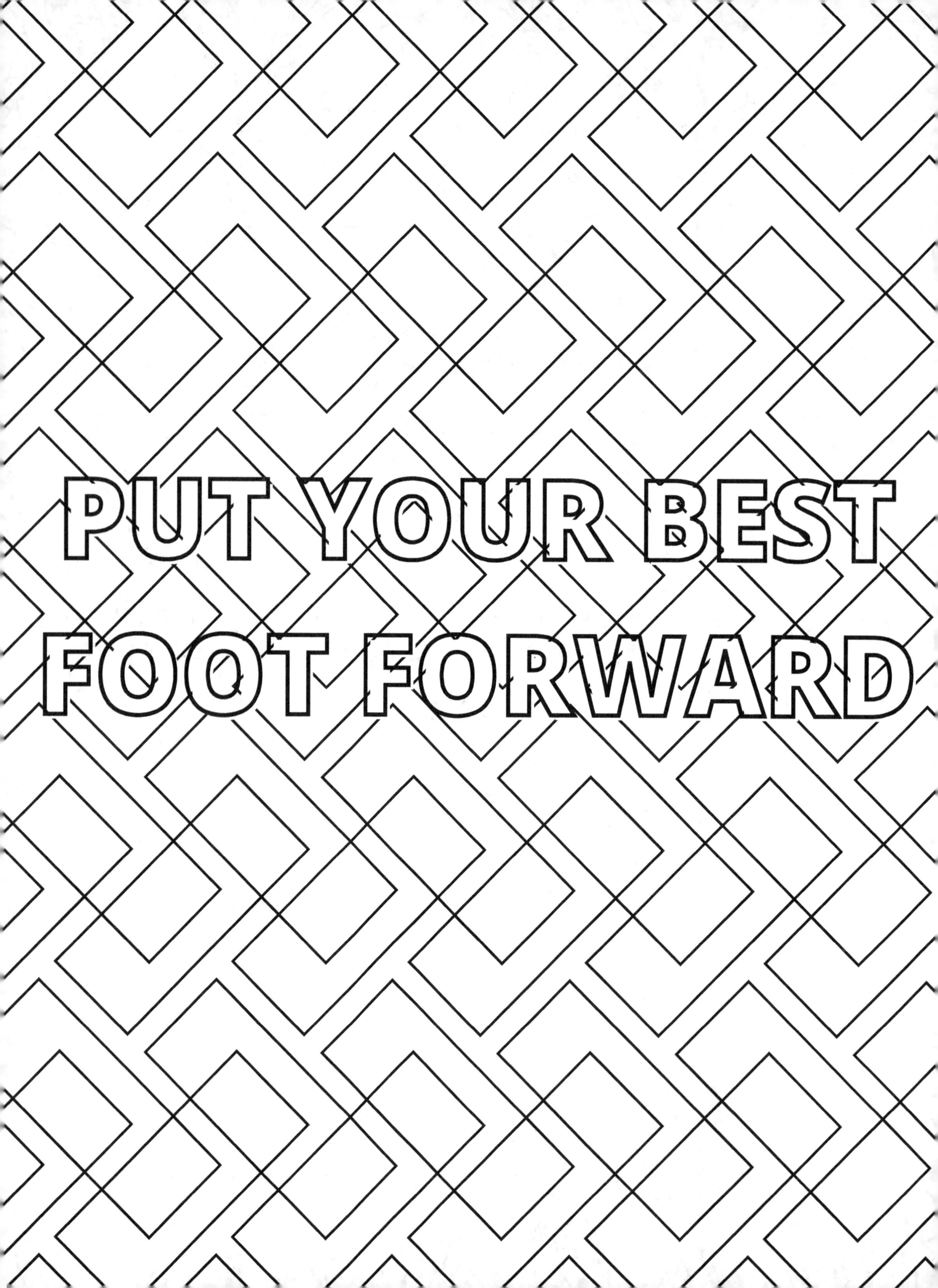

PUT YOUR BEST
FOOT FORWARD

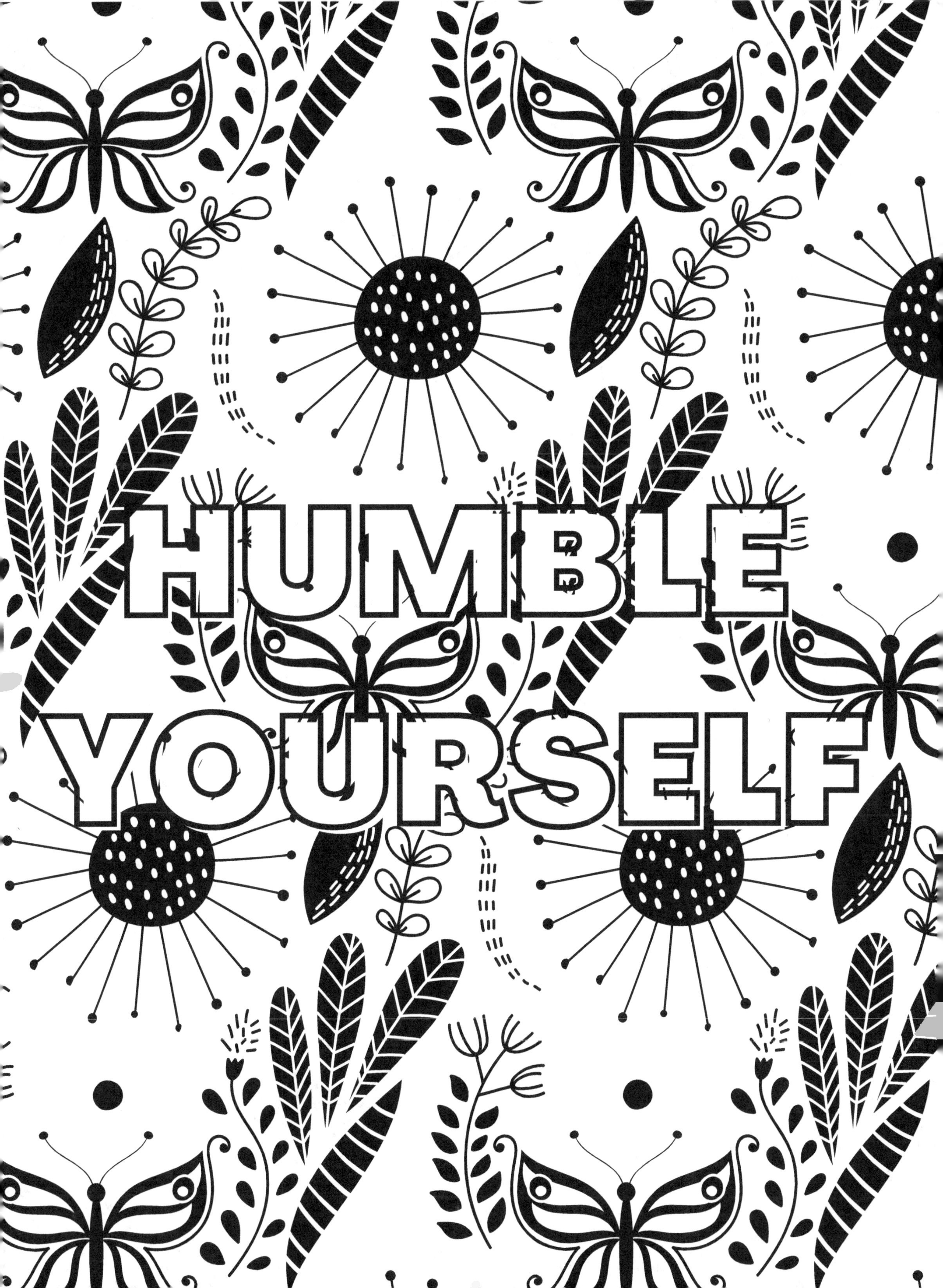

HUMBLE
YOURSELF

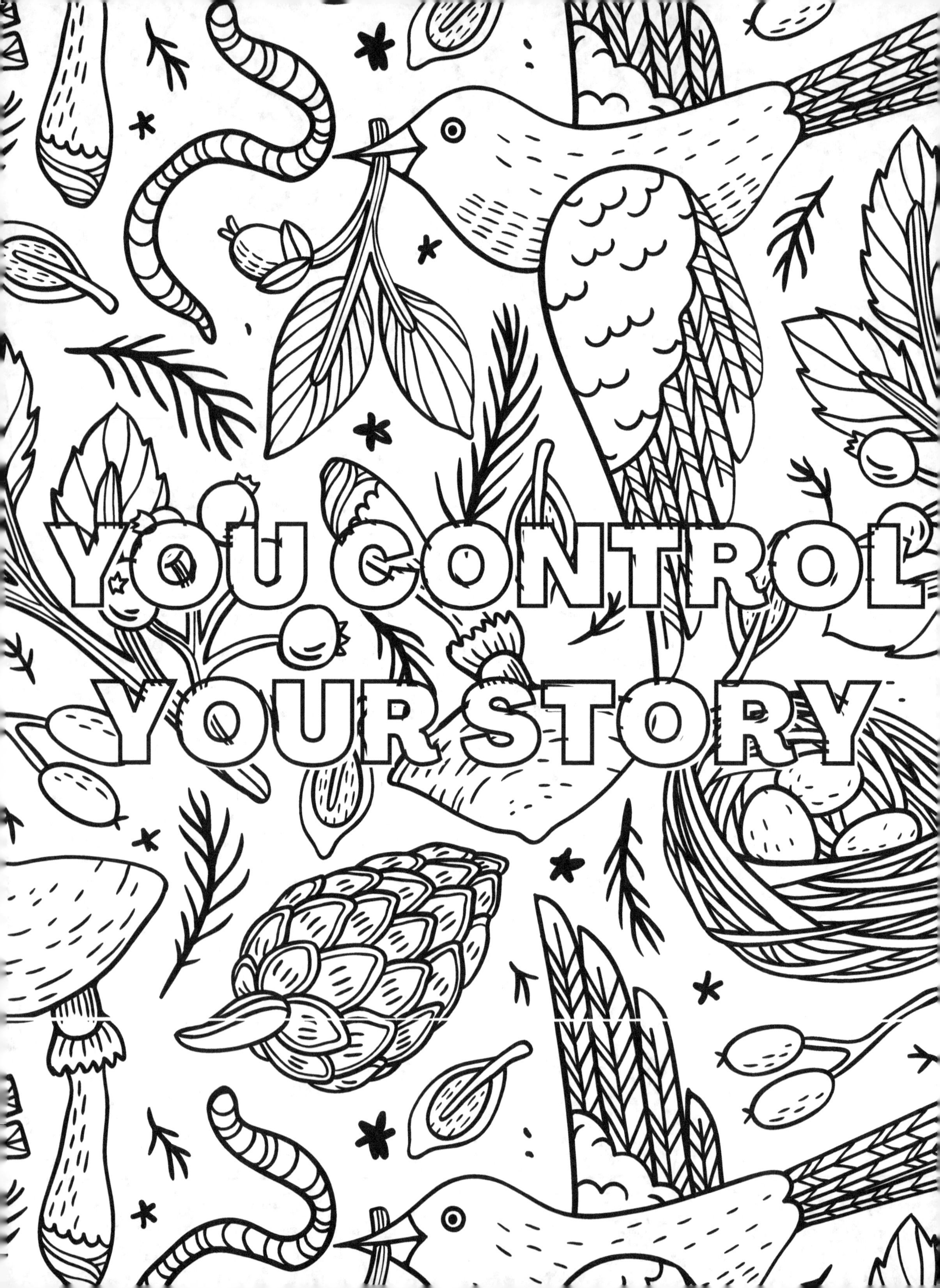

YOU CONTROL
YOUR STORY

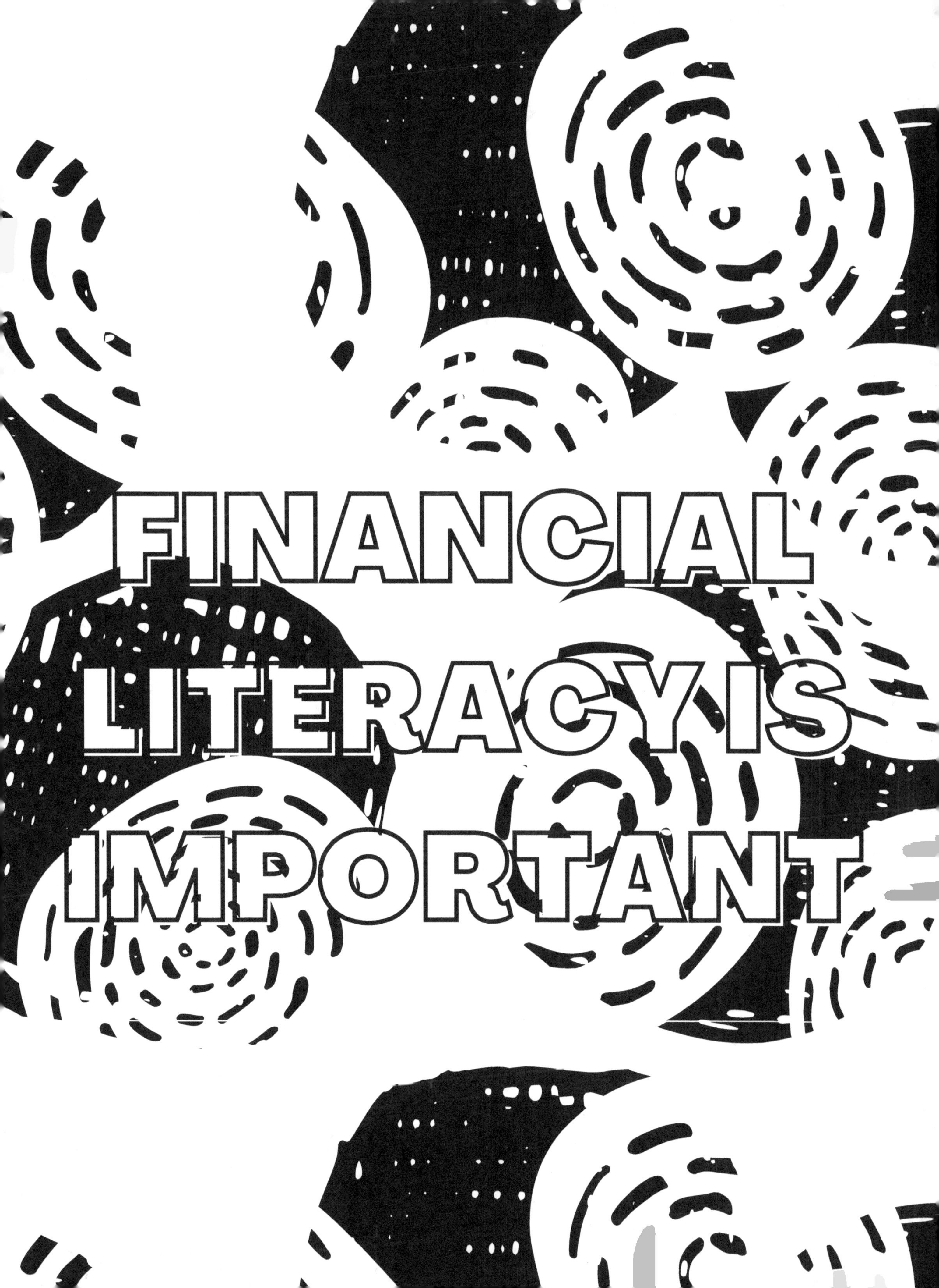

FINANCIAL
LITERACY IS
IMPORTANT

TRUST THE
PROCESS

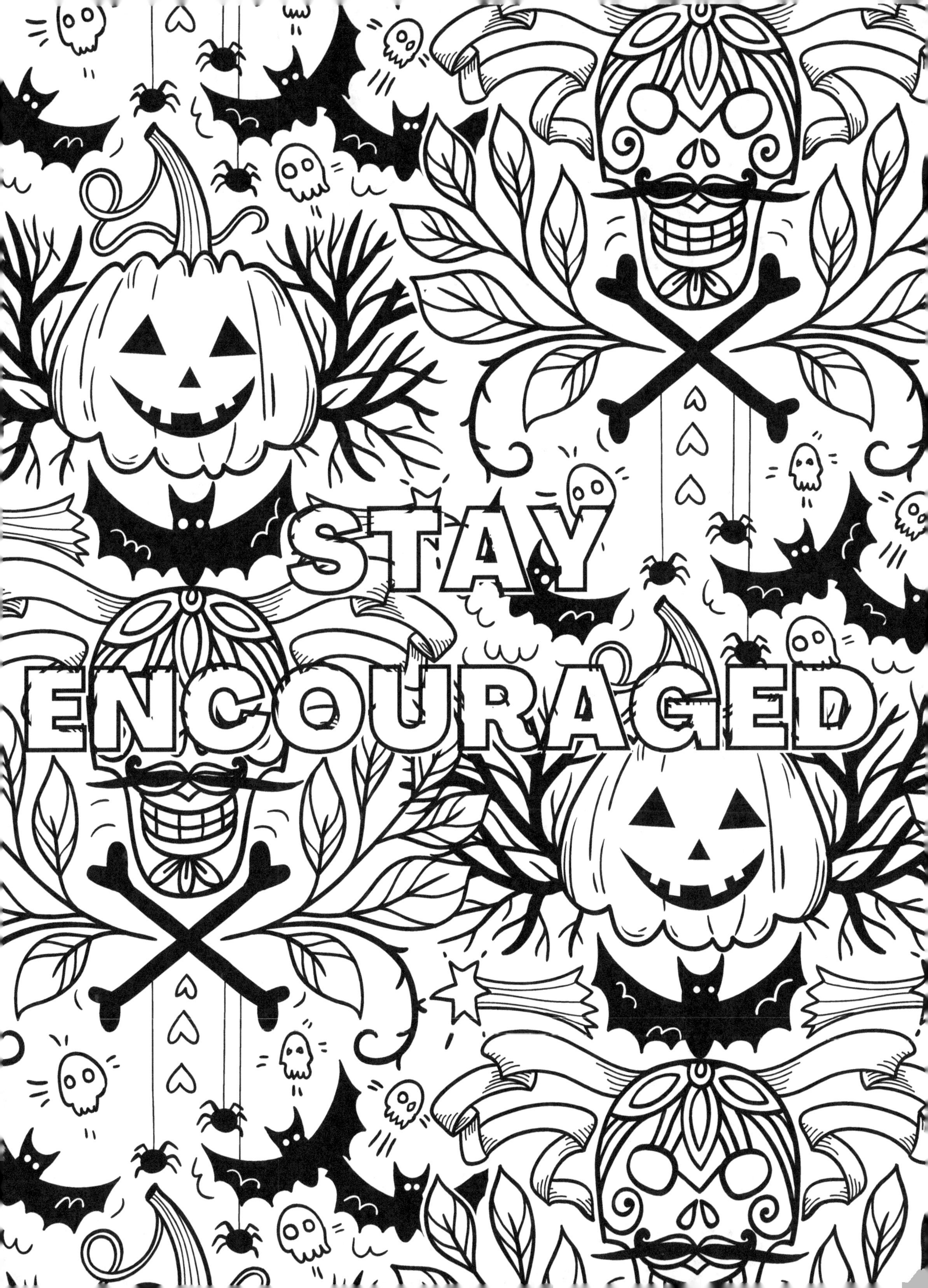
STAY
ENCOURAGED

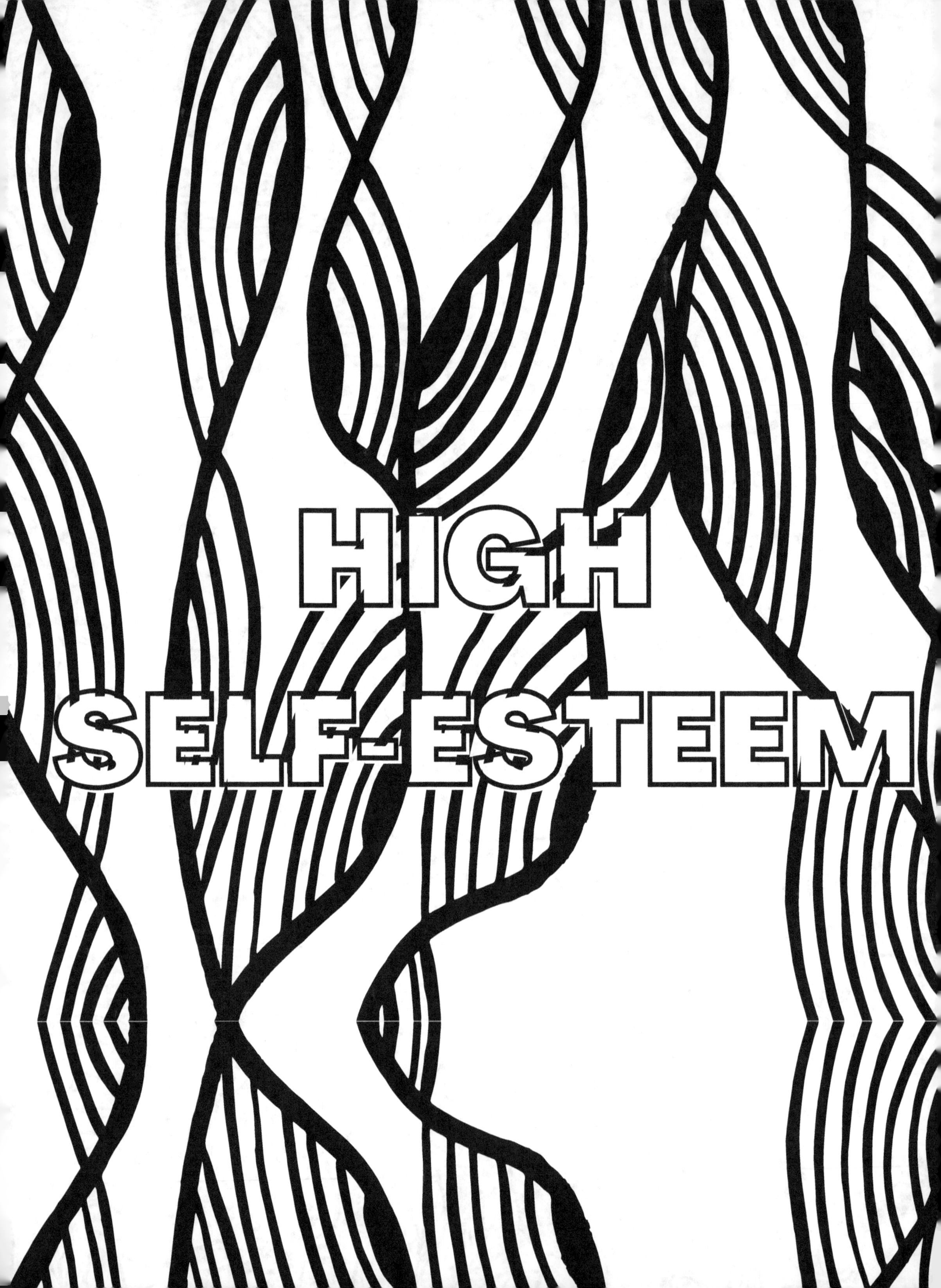

HIGH
SELF-ESTEEM

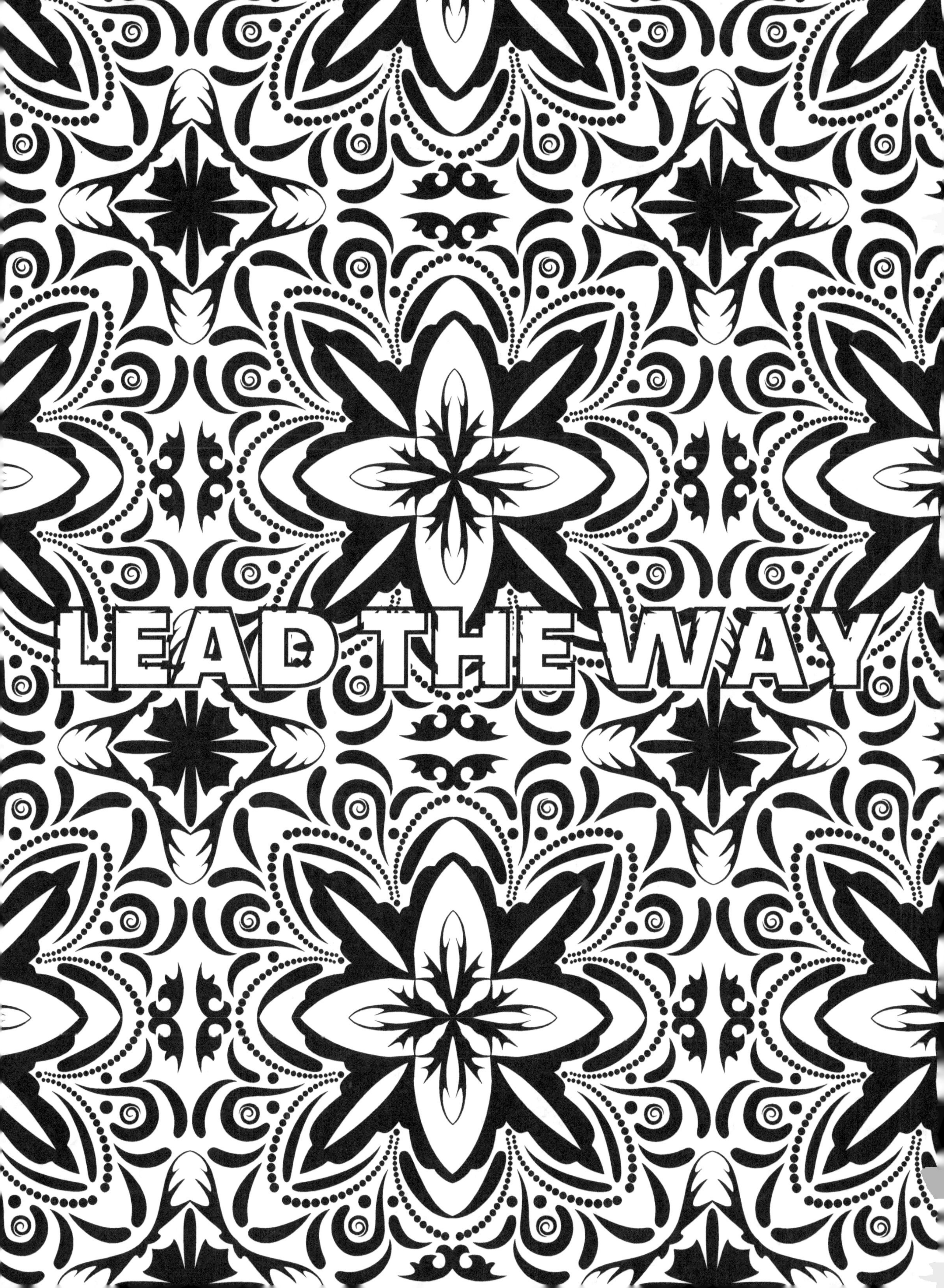

LEAD THE WAY

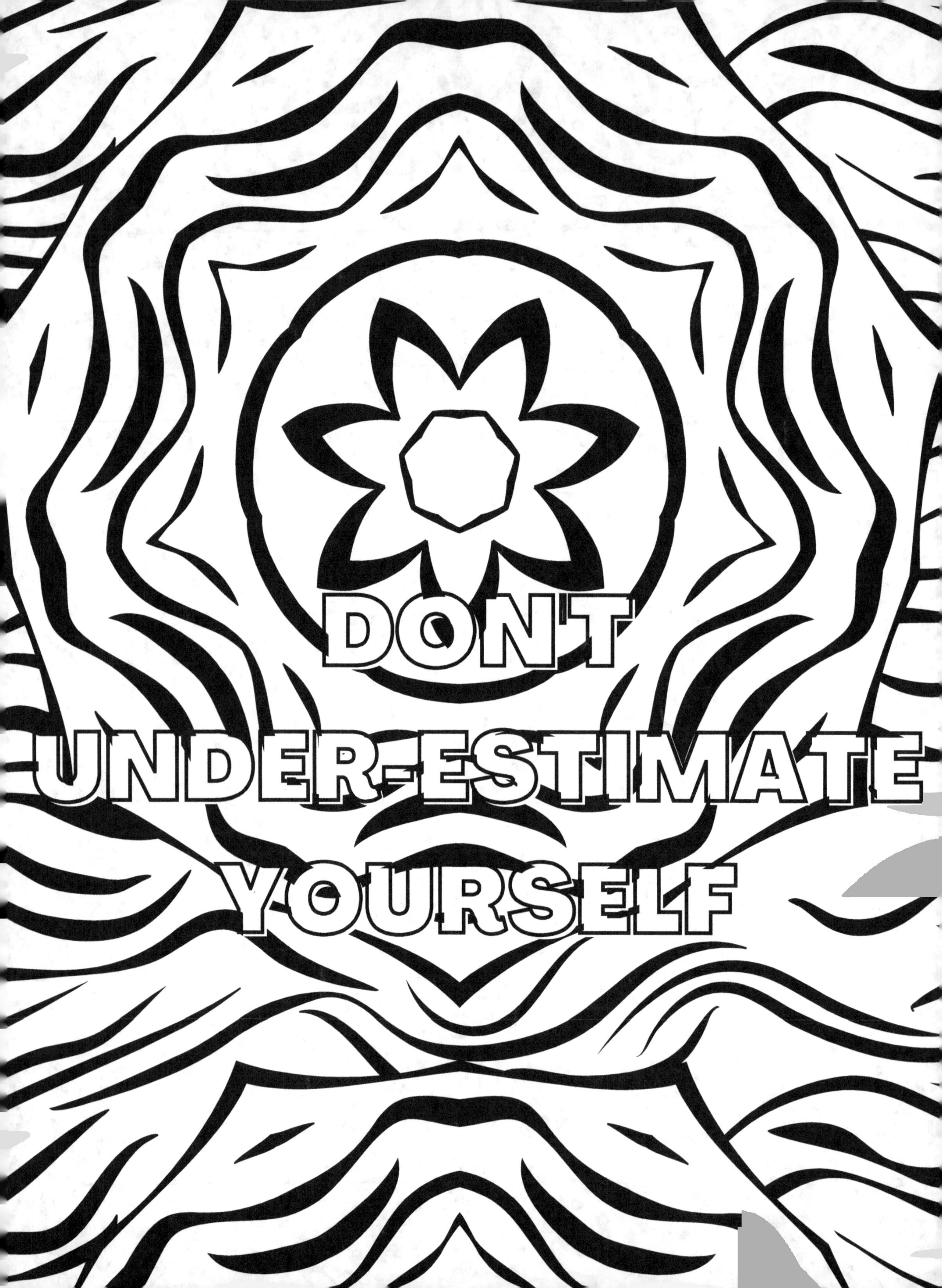

DON'T
UNDER-ESTIMATE
YOURSELF

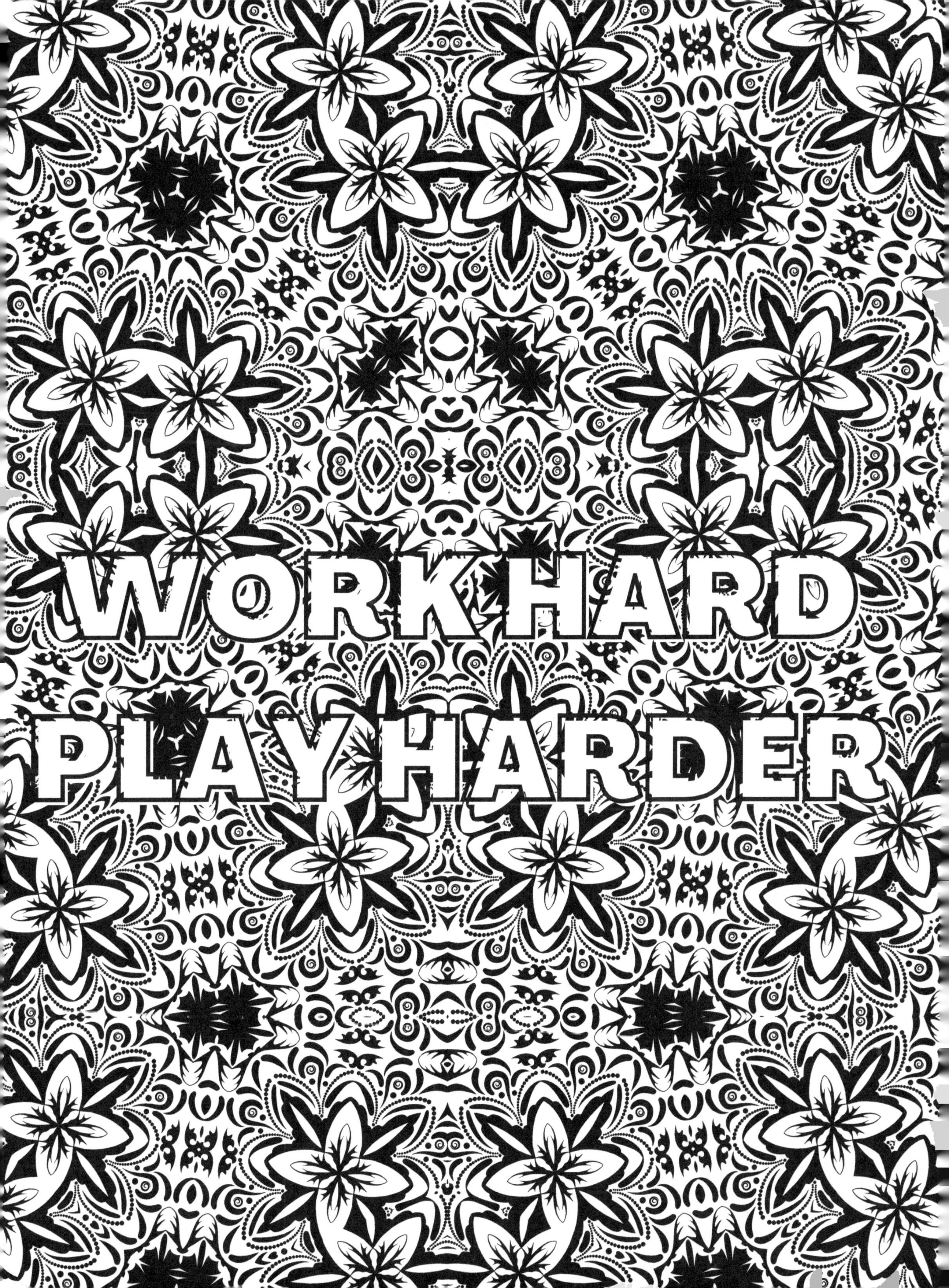

WORK HARD
PLAY HARDER

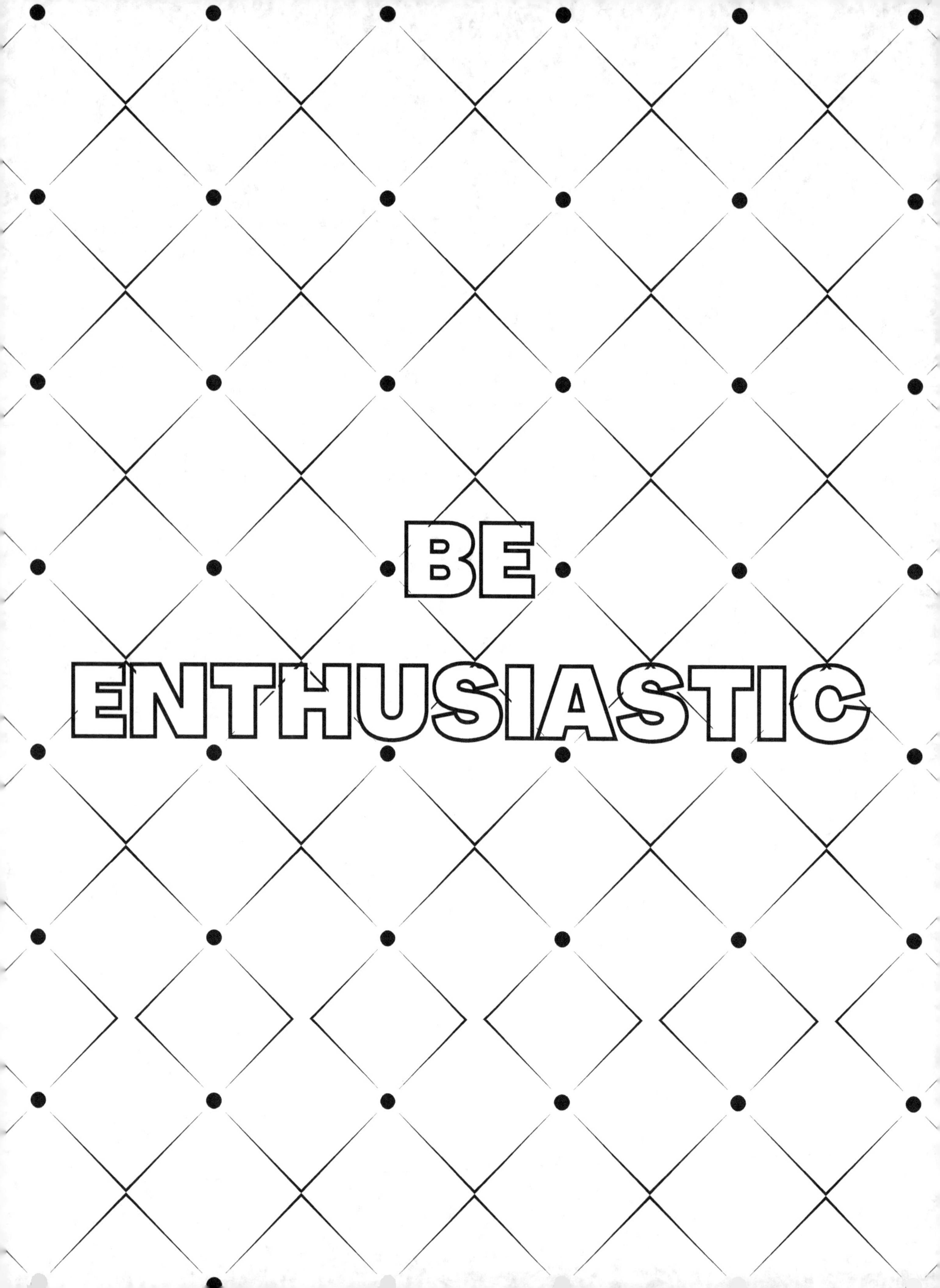

BE
ENTHUSIASTIC

CHERISH EVERY
MOMENT

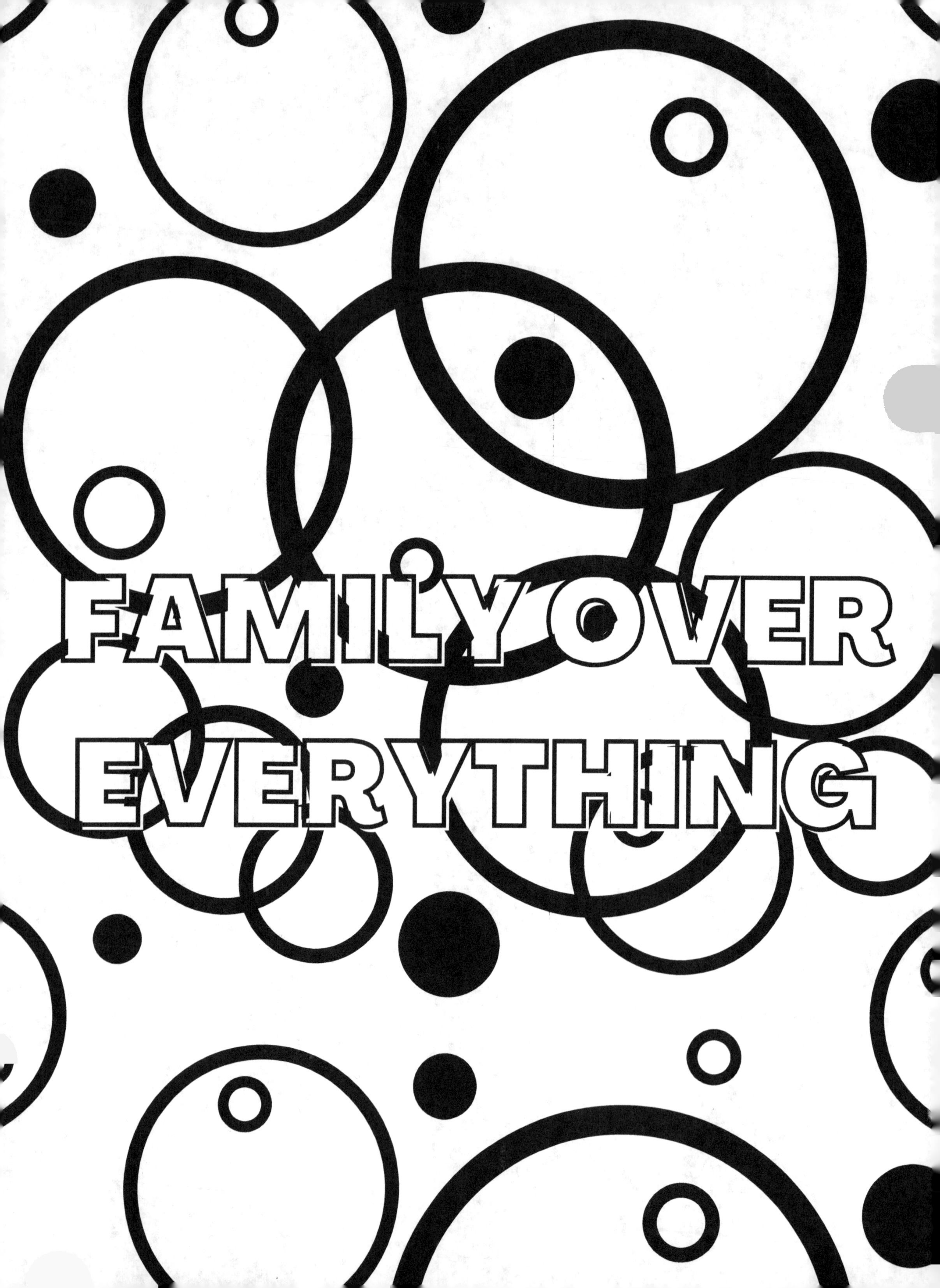

FAMILY OVER
EVERYTHING

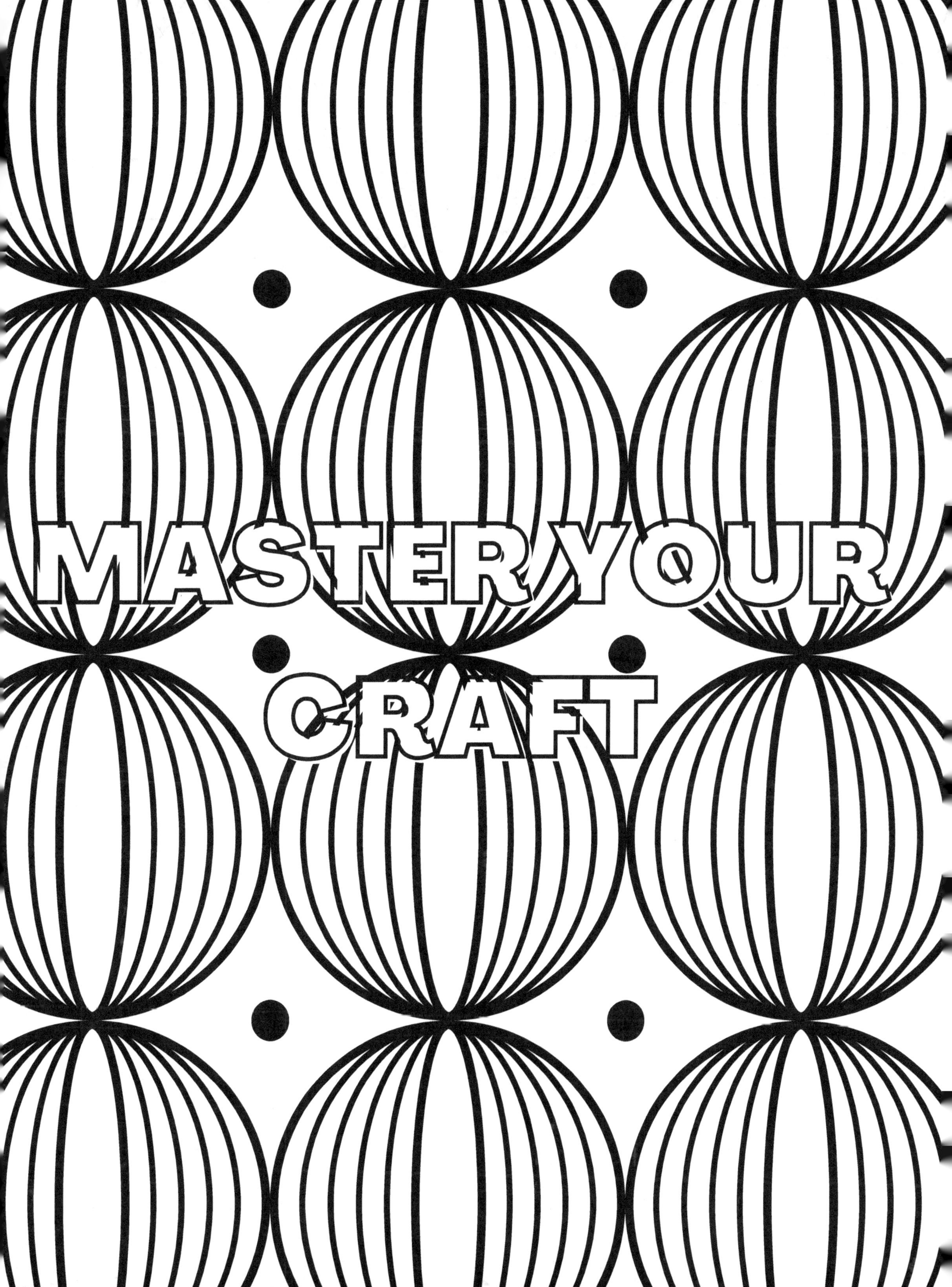

MASTER YOUR
CRAFT

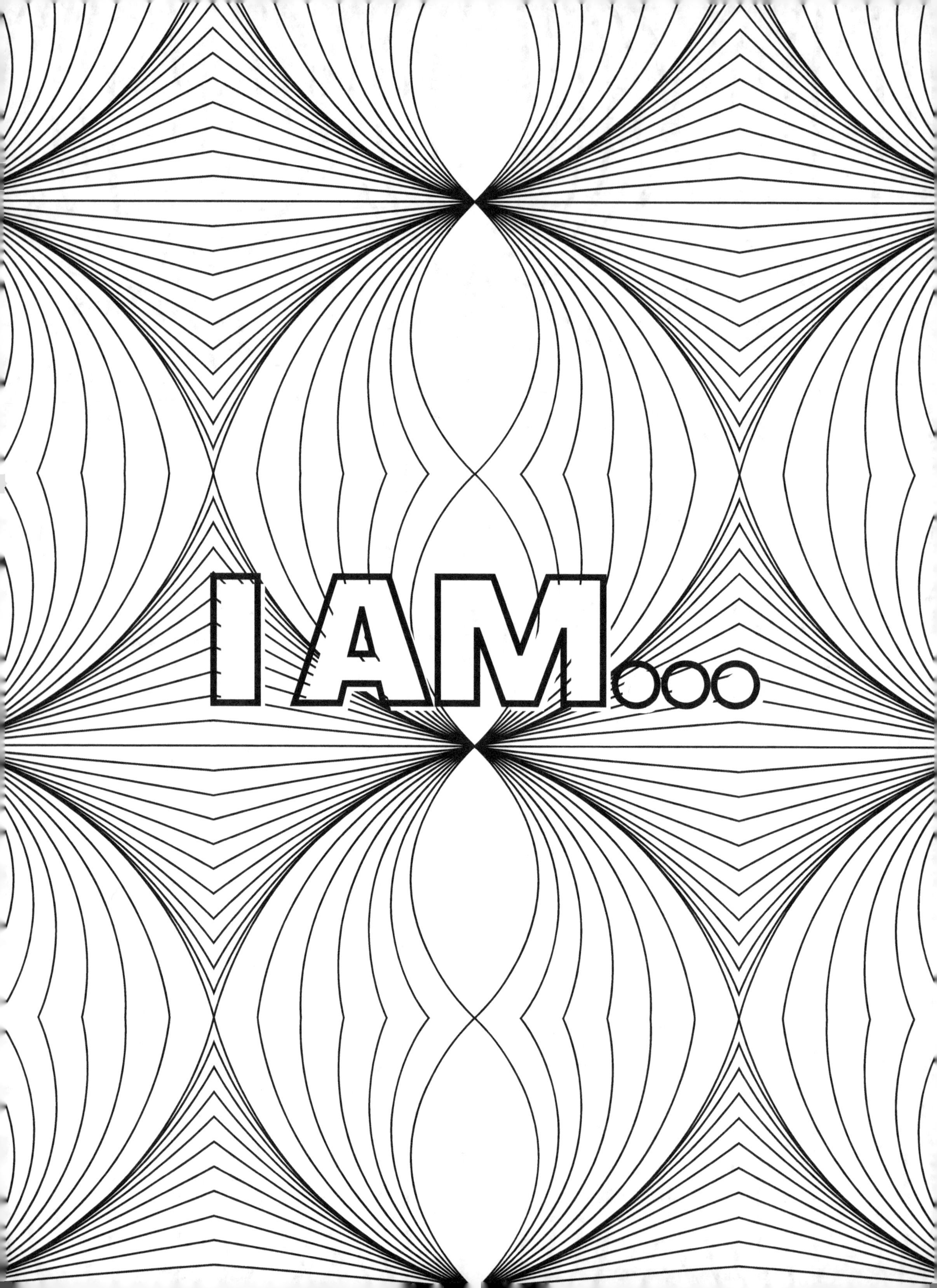

I AM...

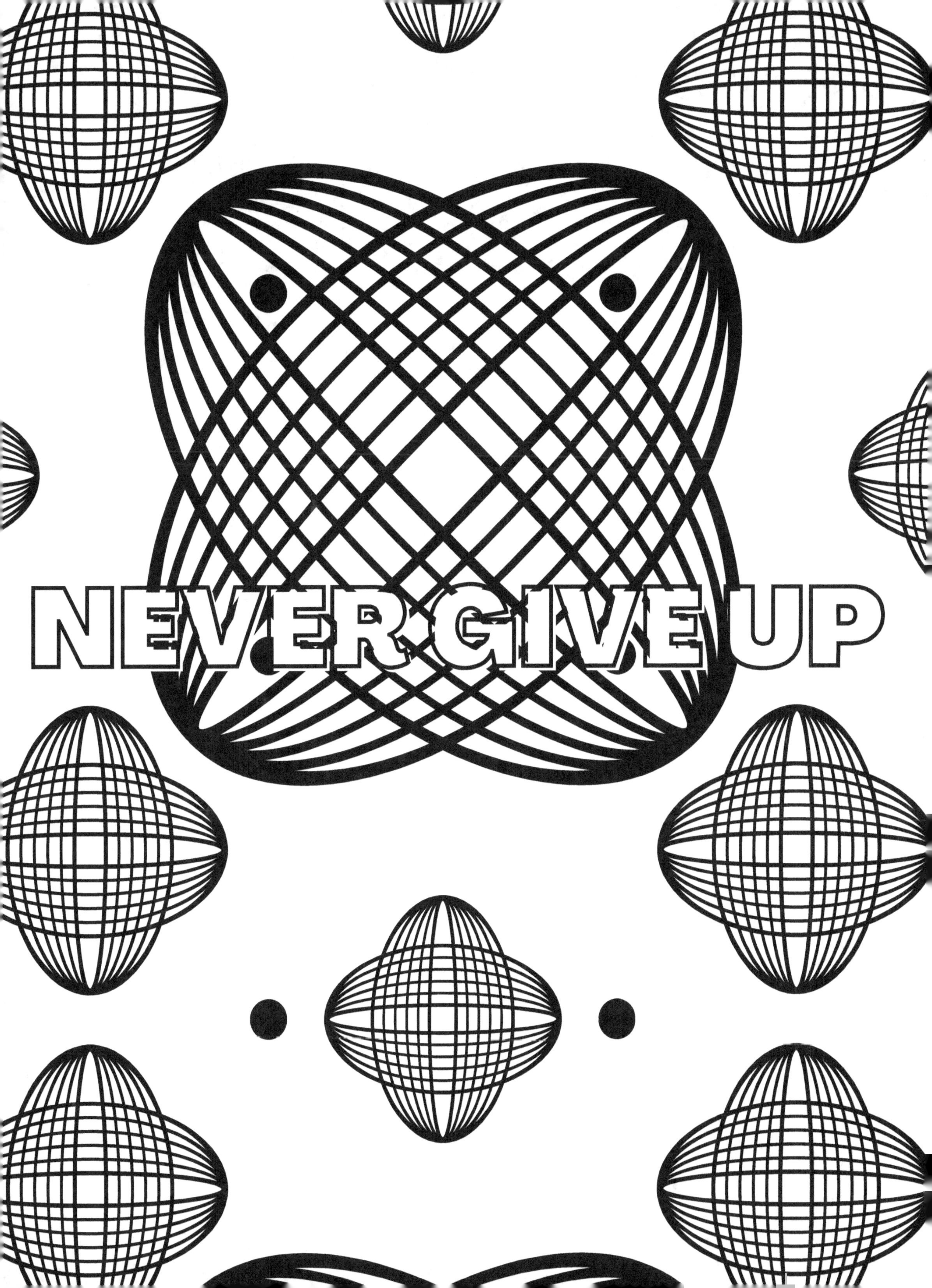
NEVER GIVE UP

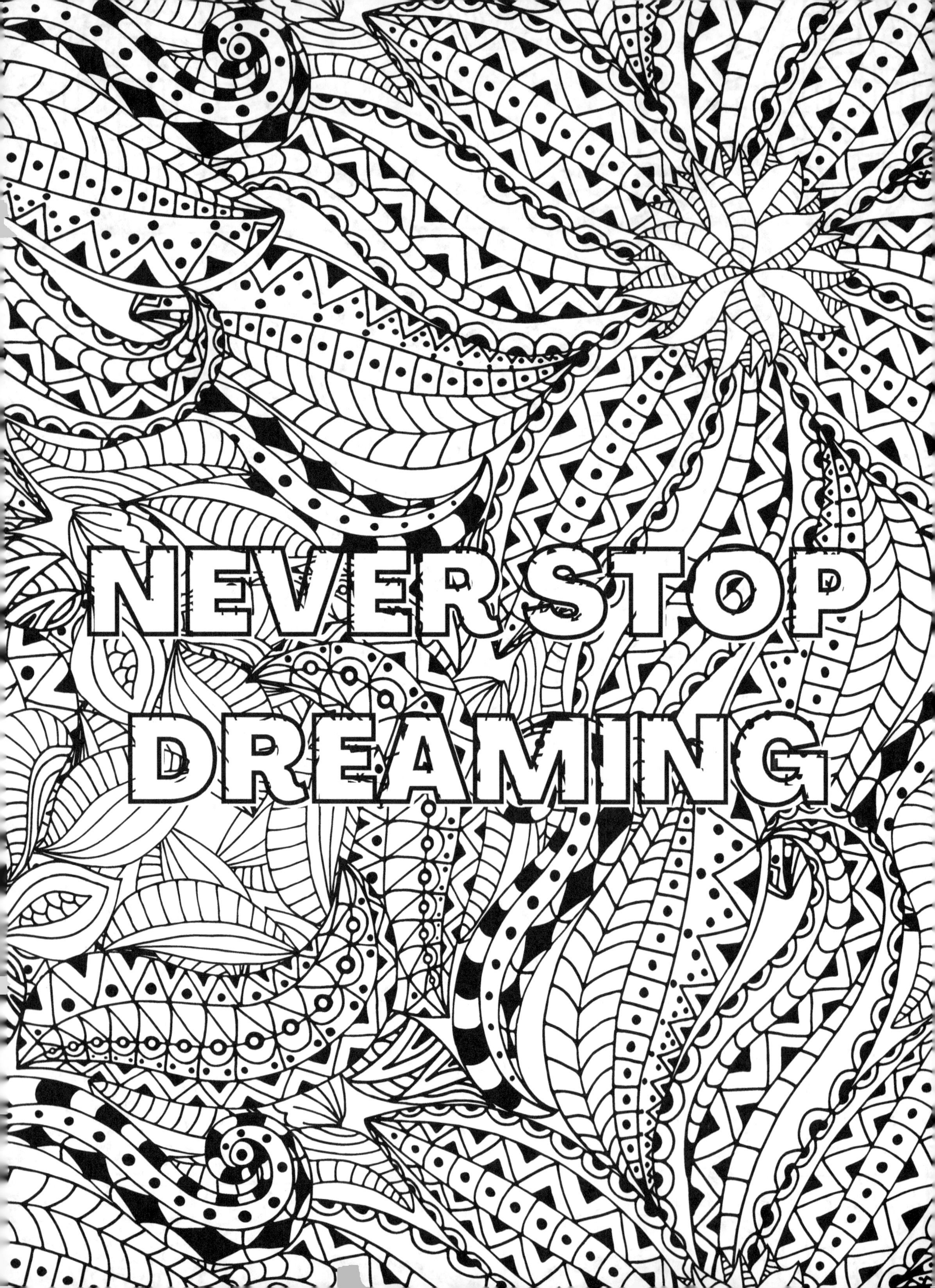

NEVER STOP
DREAMING

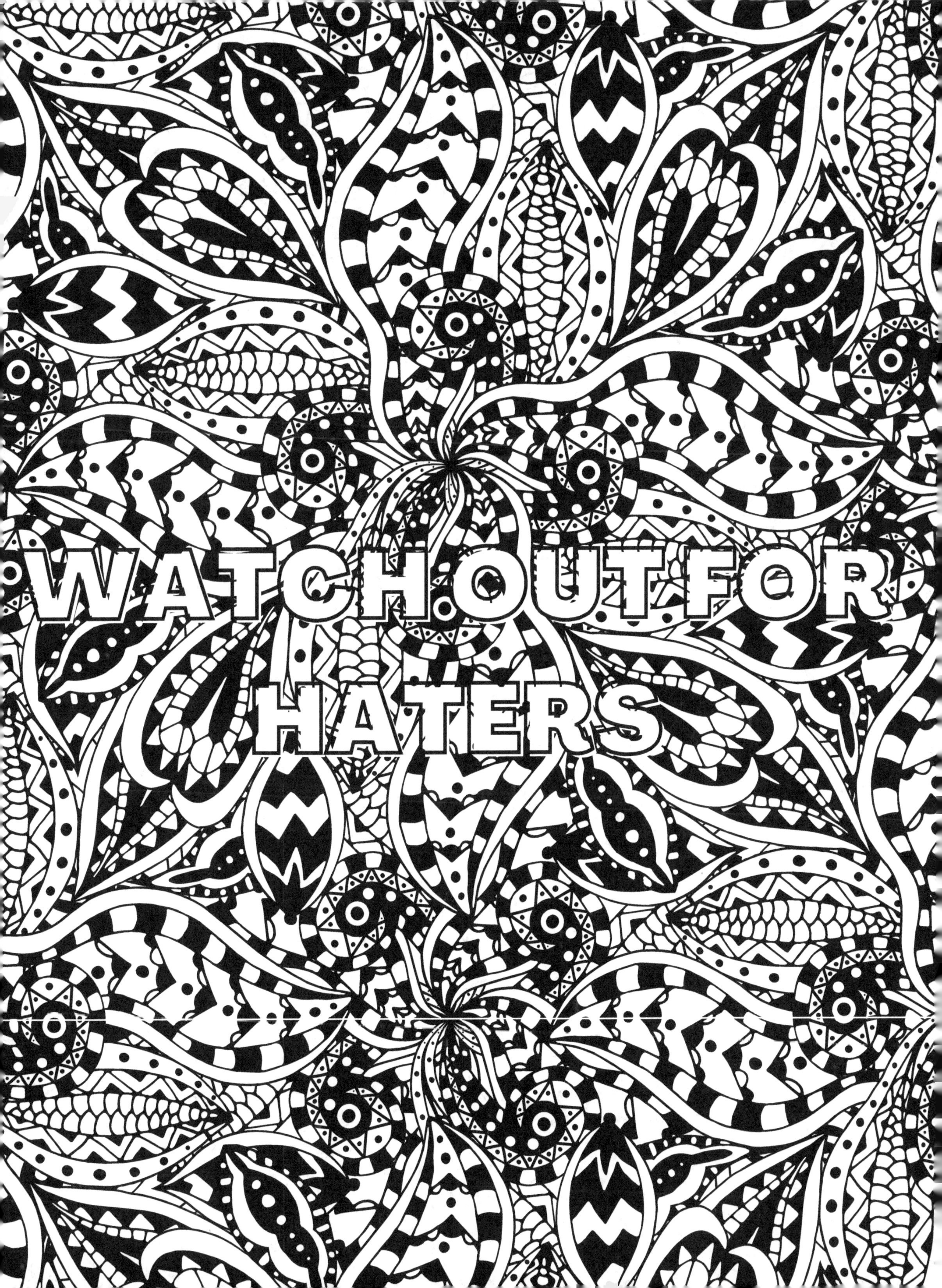

WATCH OUT FOR
HATERS

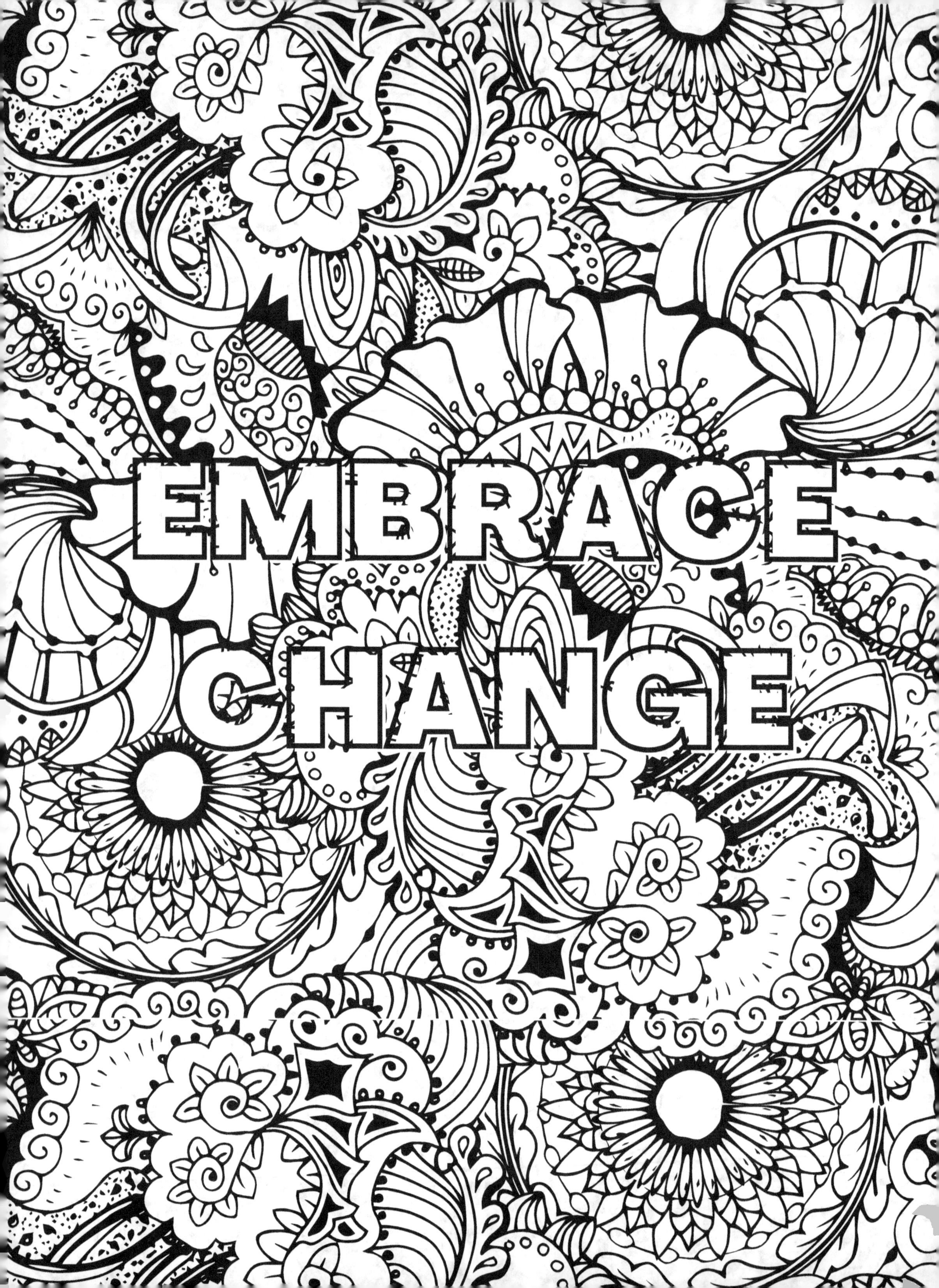

EMBRACE
CHANGE

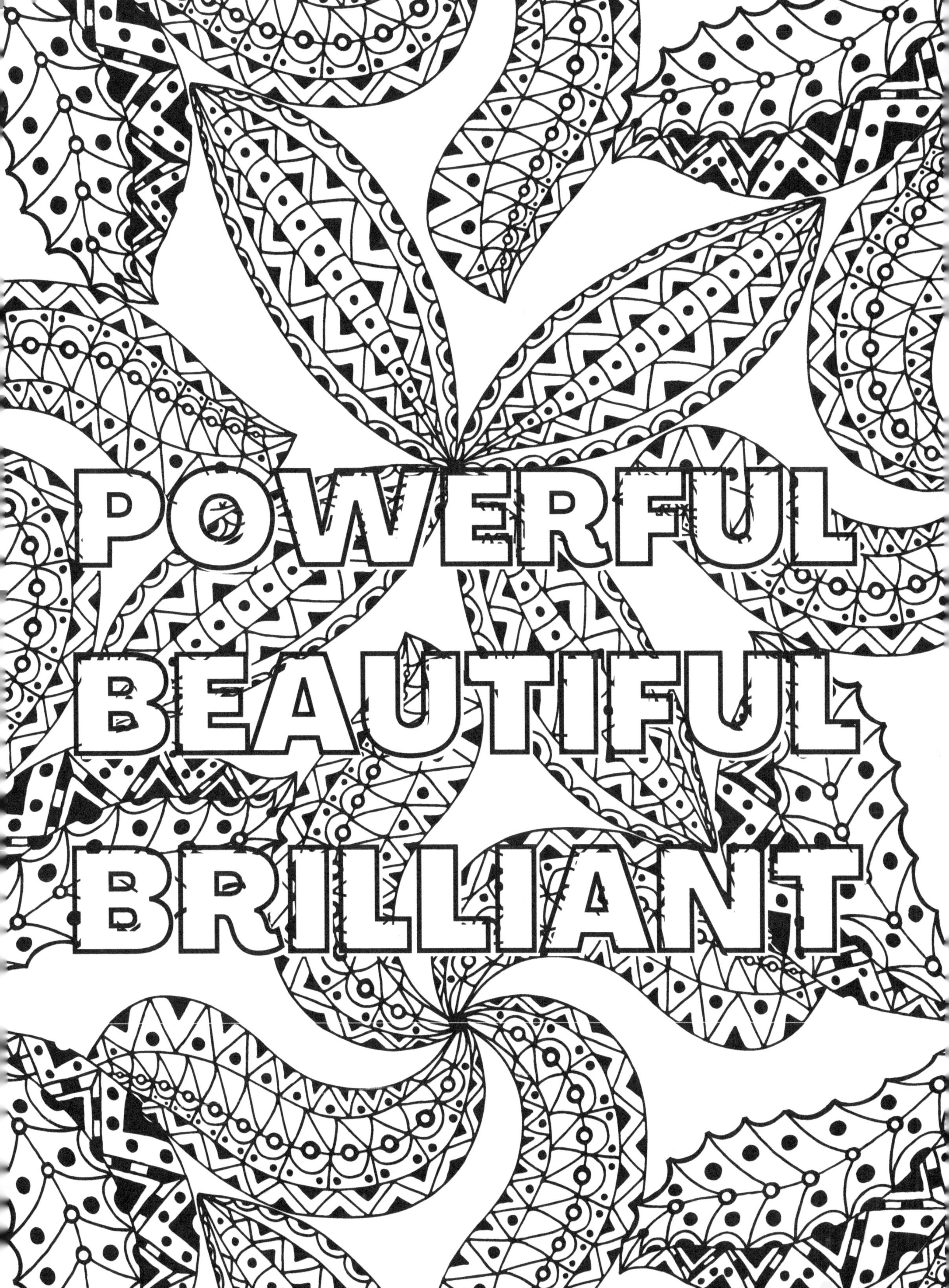

POWERFUL
BEAUTIFUL
BRILLIANT

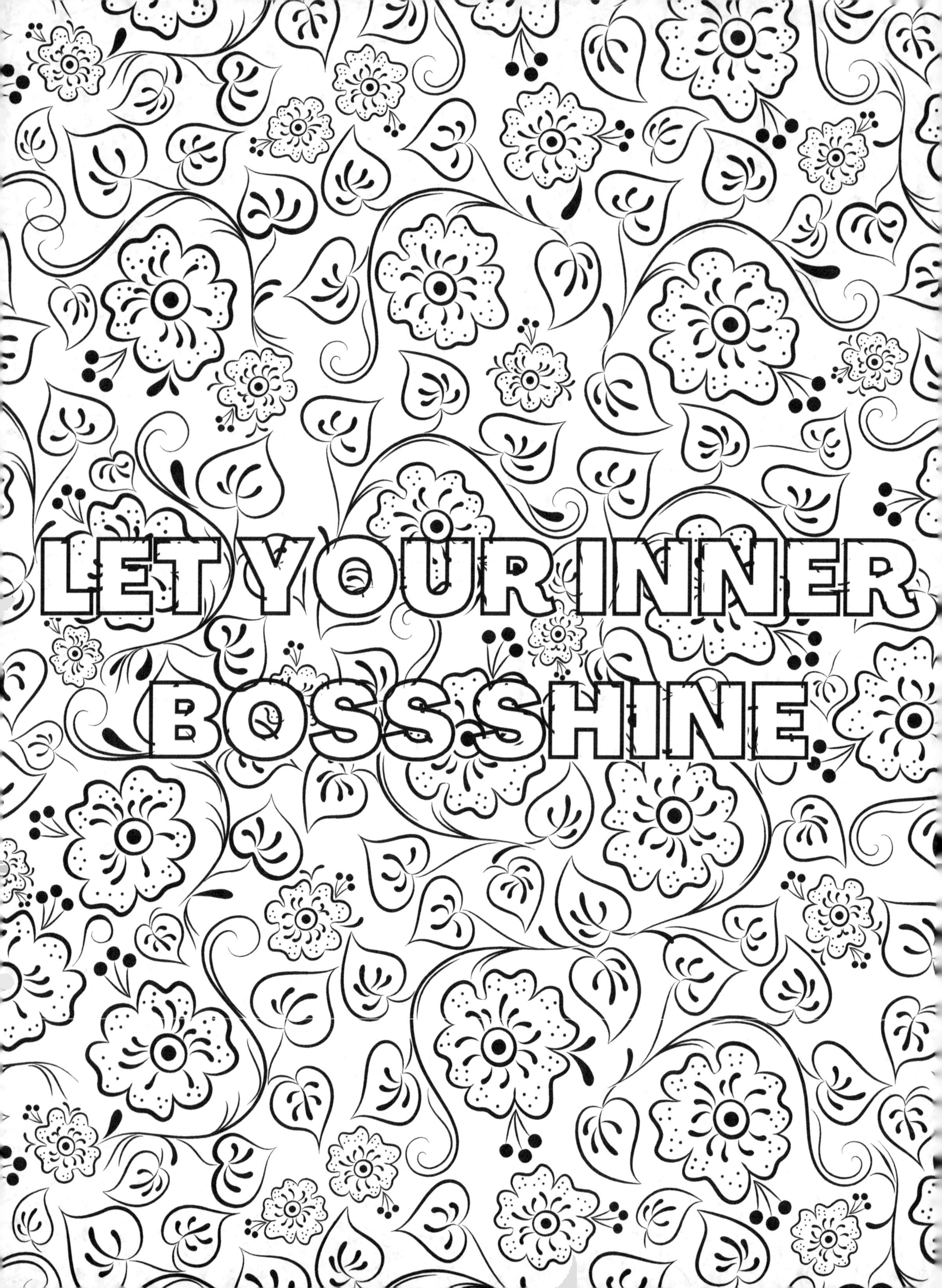

LET YOUR INNER
BOSS SHINE

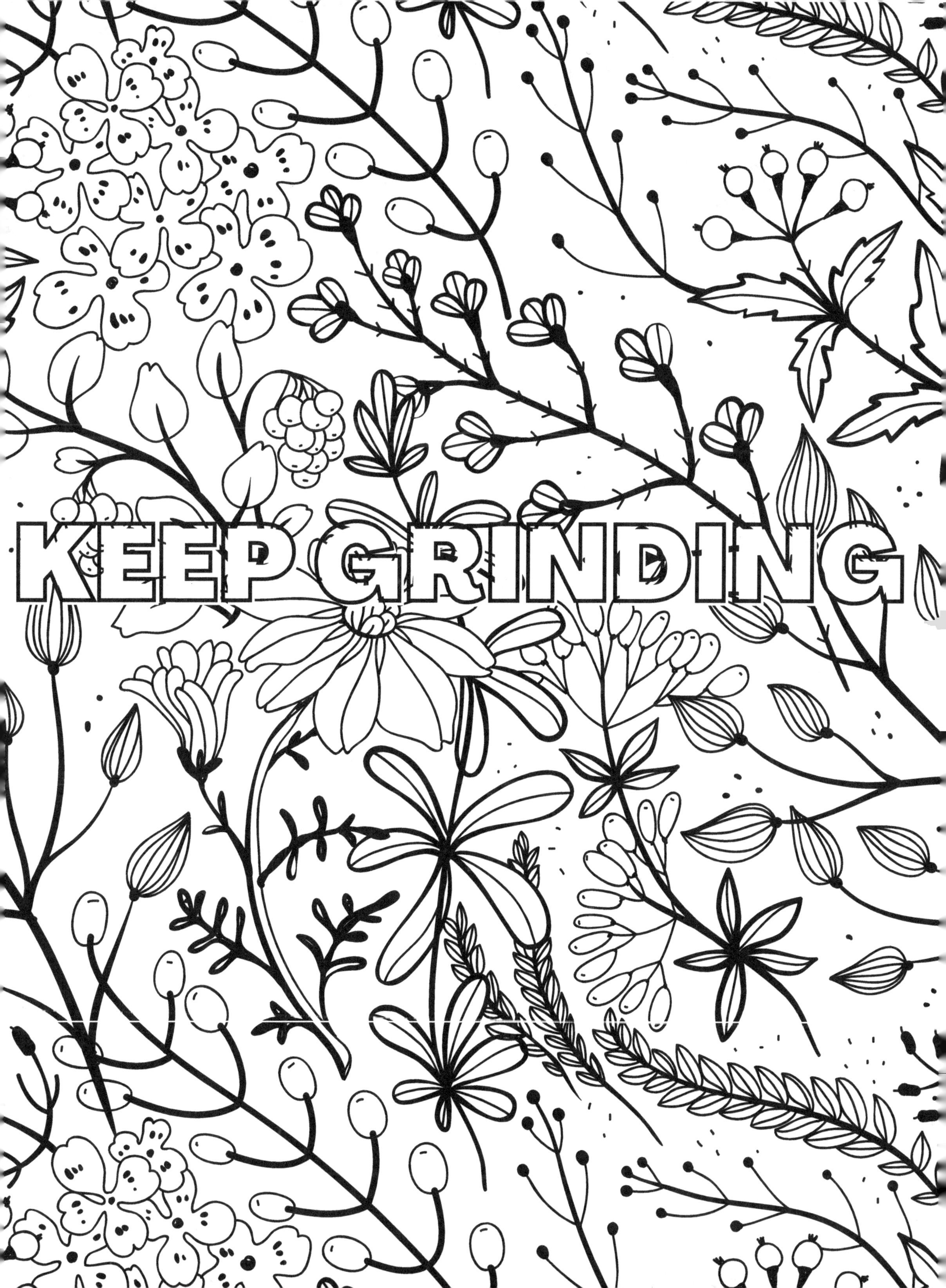

KEEP GRINDING

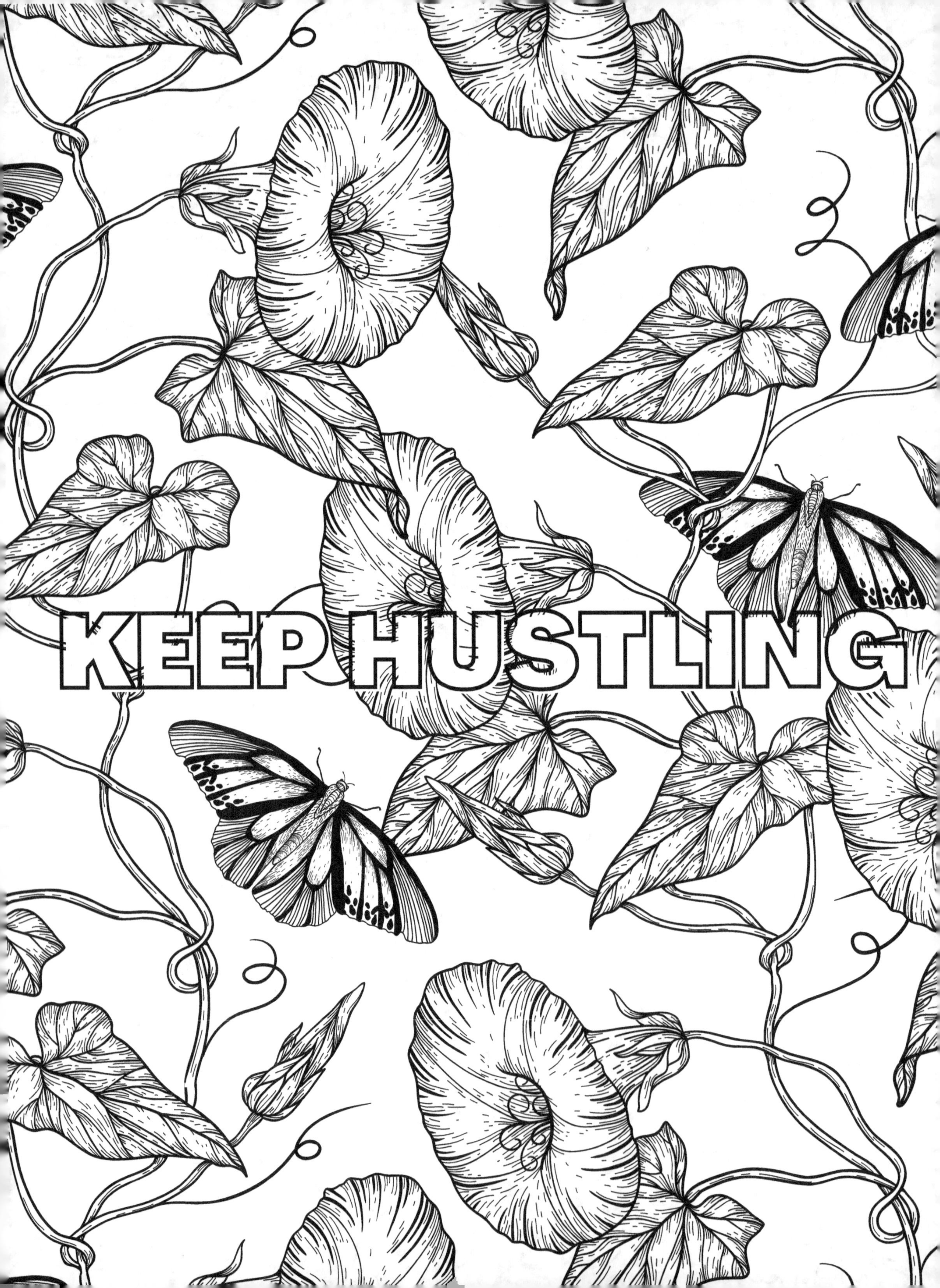

KEEP HUSTLING

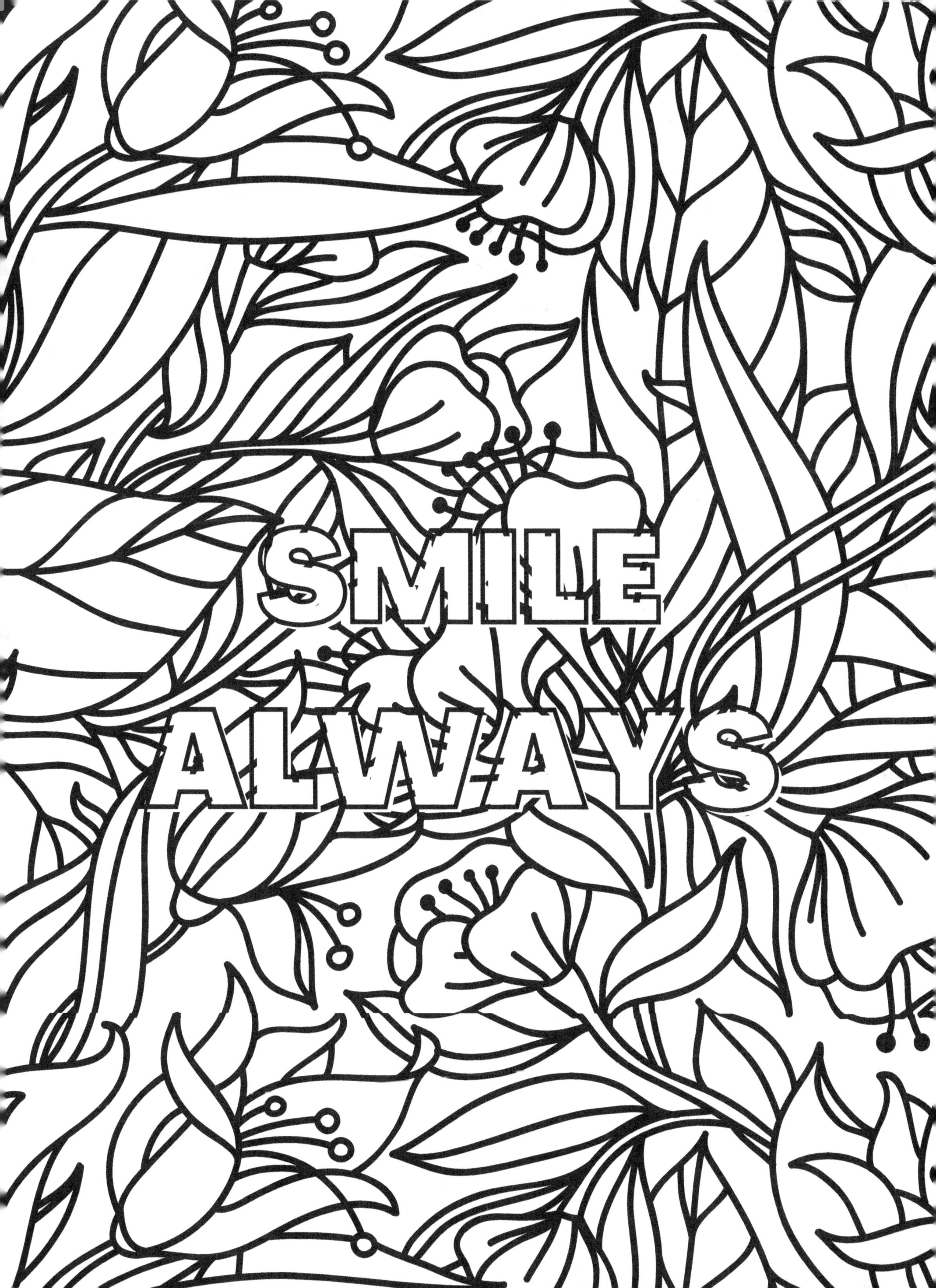

SMILE
ALWAYS

TAKE THE RISK
OR
LOSE THE CHANCE

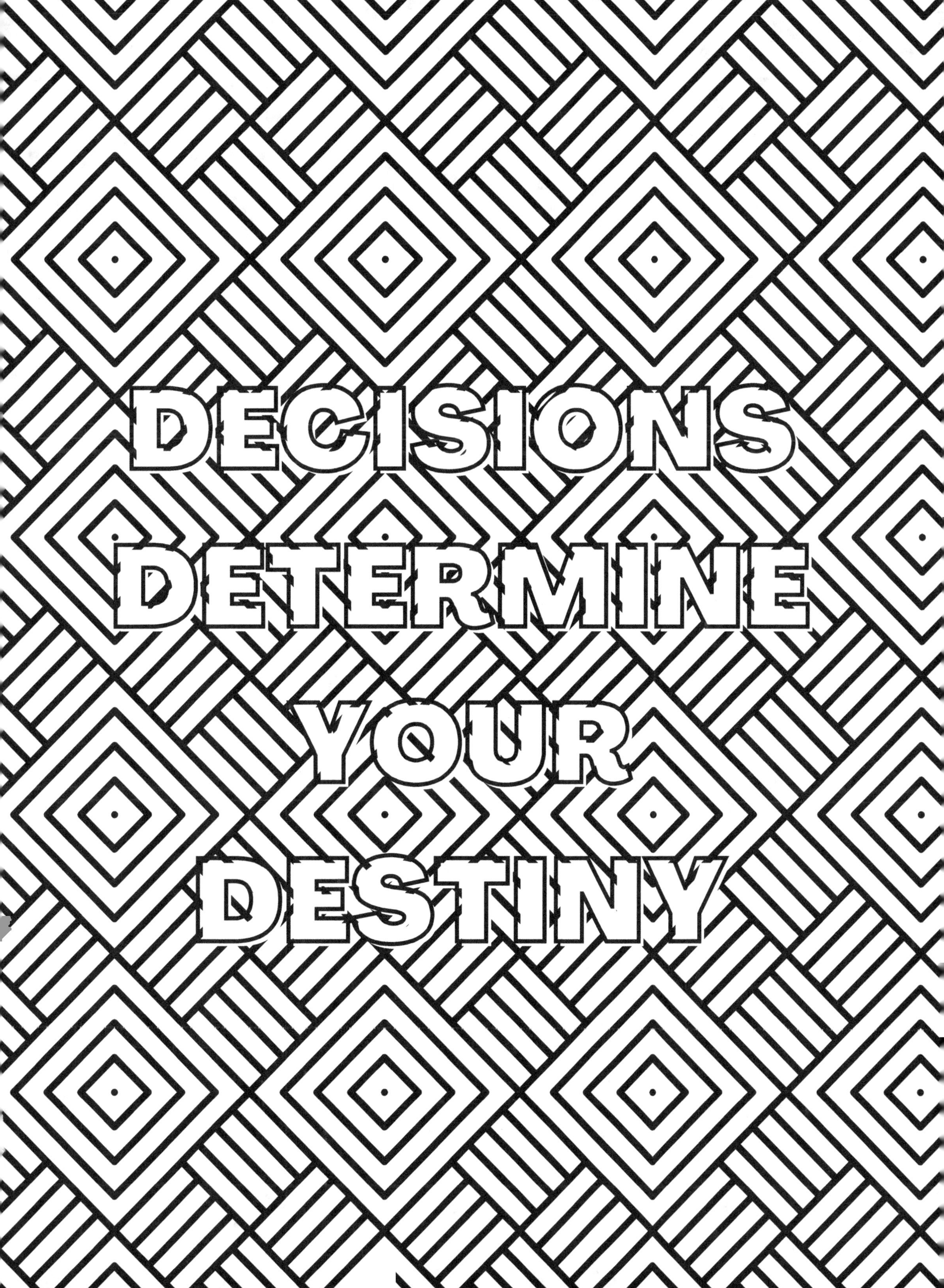

DECISIONS
DETERMINE
YOUR
DESTINY

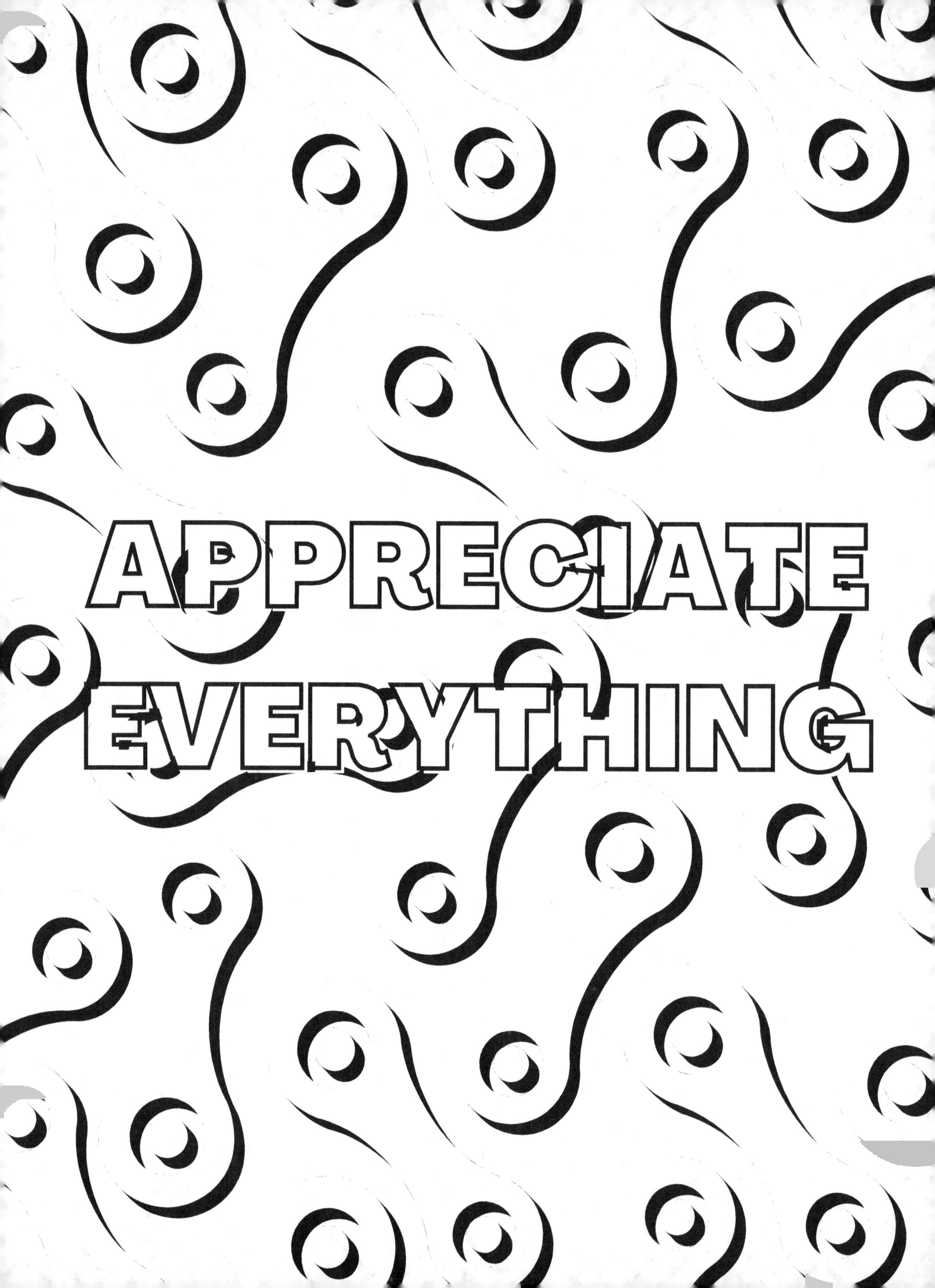

APPRECIATE
EVERYTHING

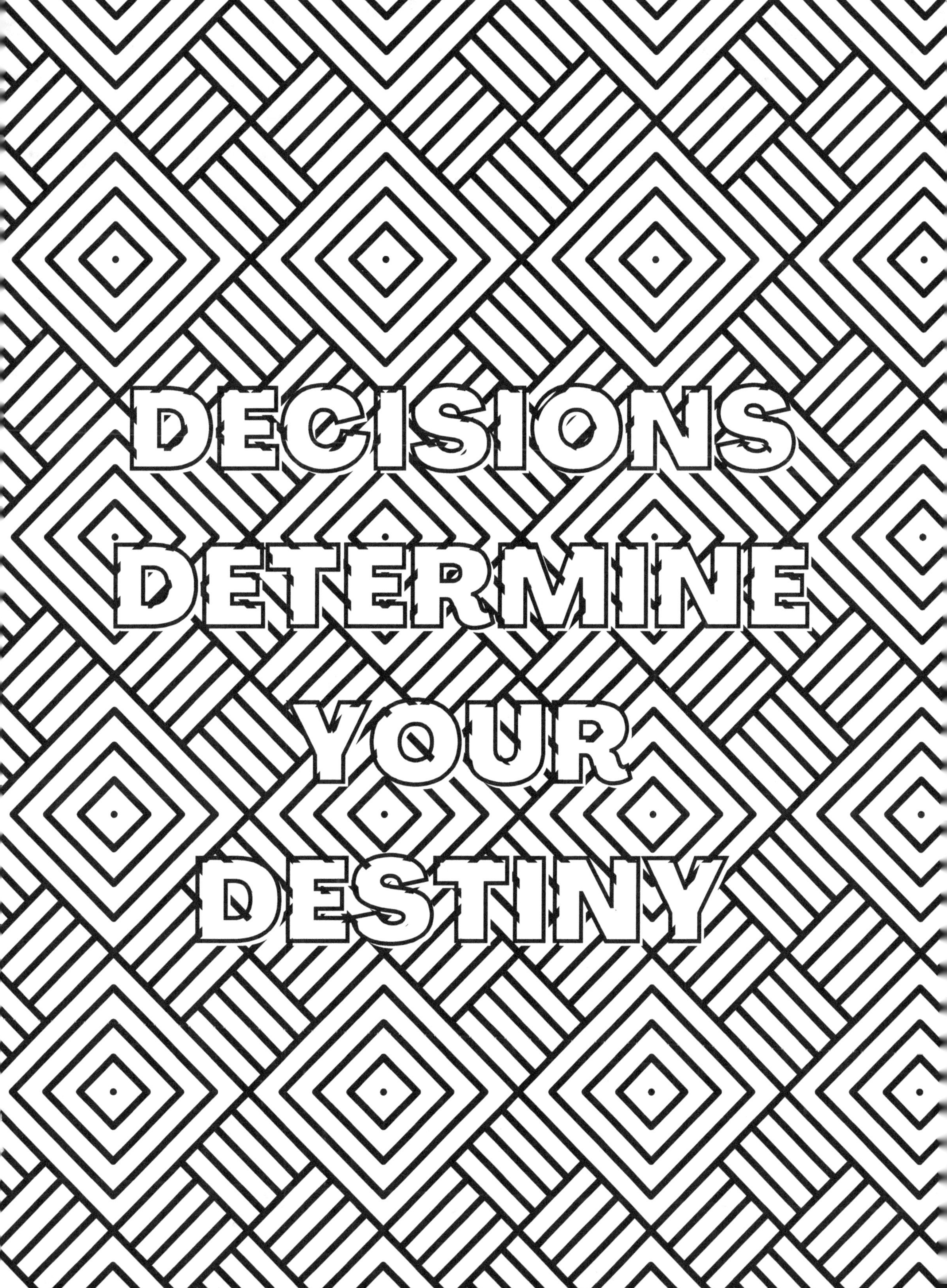

DECISIONS
DETERMINE
YOUR
DESTINY

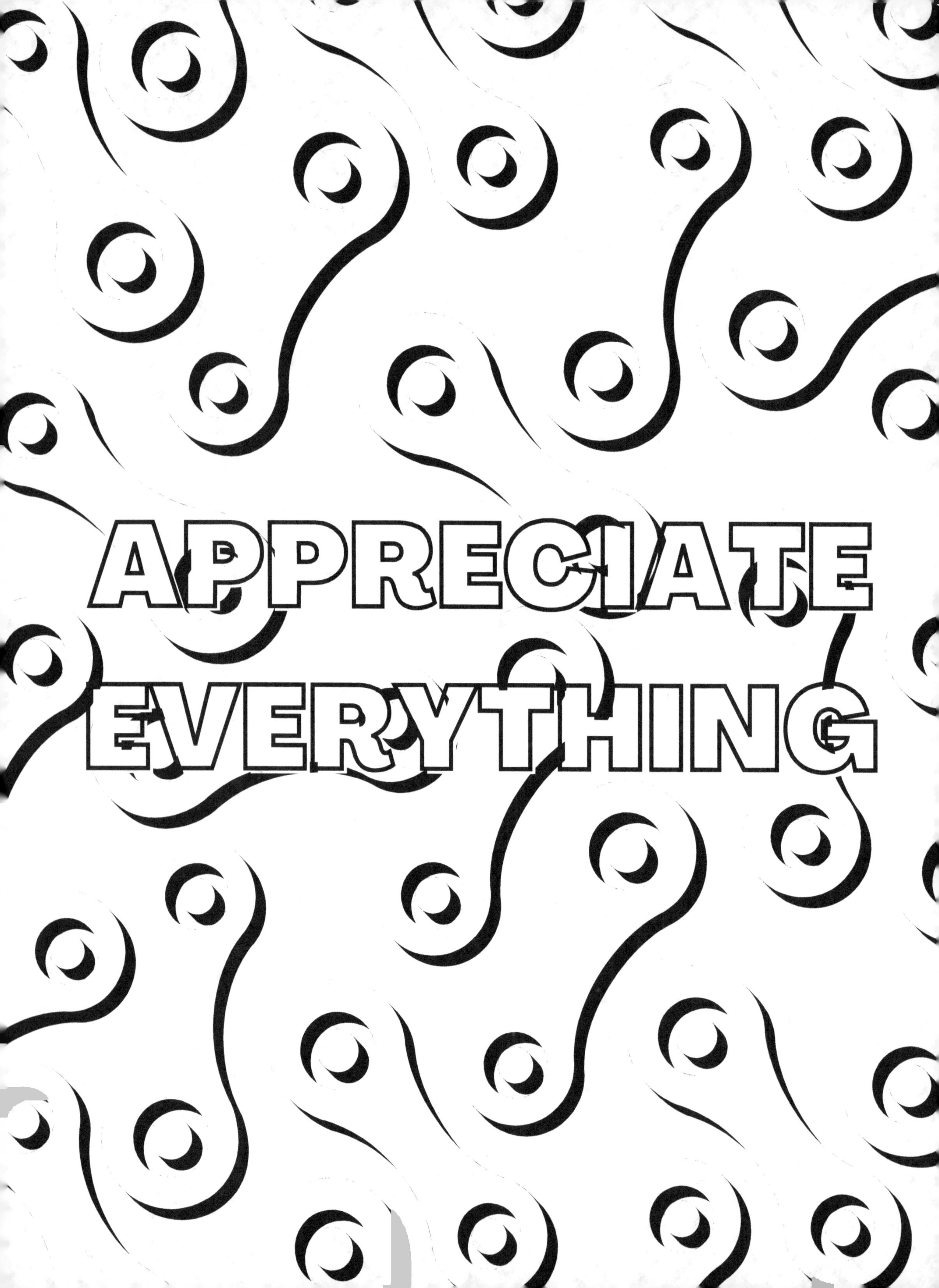

APPRECIATE
EVERYTHING

PROVE THEM
WRONG

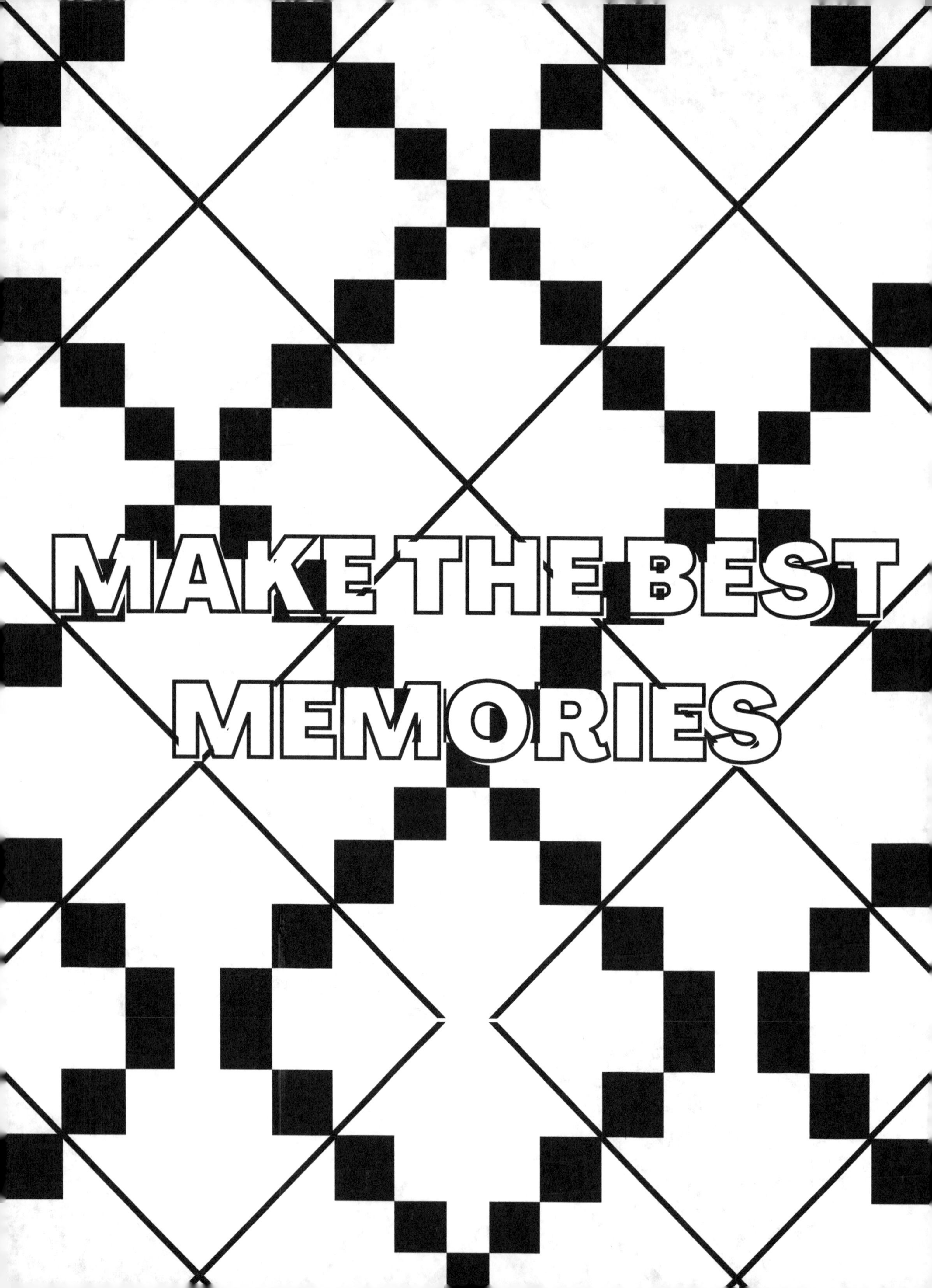

MAKE THE BEST
MEMORIES

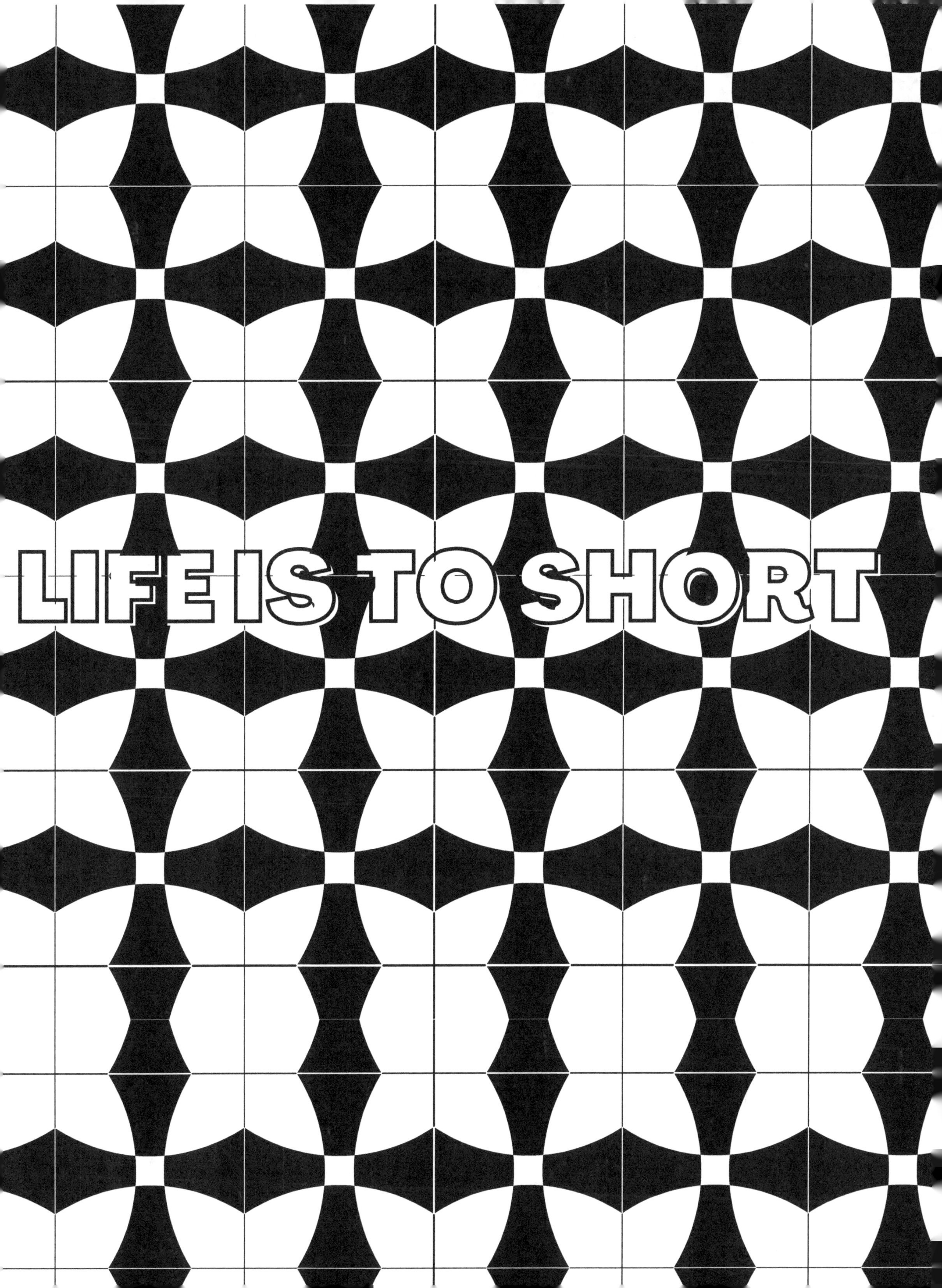
LIFE IS TO SHORT